Nova Scotia House
A Novel
Charlie Porter

PARTICULAR BOOKS
an imprint of
PENGUIN BOOKS

PARTICULAR BOOKS

UK | USA | Canada | Ireland | Australia
India | New Zealand | South Africa

Particular Books is part of the Penguin Random House group of companies whose addresses can be found at global.penguinrandomhouse.com

Penguin Random House UK,
One Embassy Gardens, 8 Viaduct Gardens, London SW11 7BW

penguin.co.uk

First published 2025
008

Copyright © Charlie Porter, 2025
The moral right of the author has been asserted

Images reproduced by courtesy of the UK AIDS Memorial Quilt Partnership

Penguin Random House values and supports copyright.
Copyright fuels creativity, encourages diverse voices, promotes freedom of expression and supports a vibrant culture. Thank you for purchasing an authorized edition of this book and for respecting intellectual property laws by not reproducing, scanning or distributing any part of it by any means without permission. You are supporting authors and enabling Penguin Random House to continue to publish books for everyone.
No part of this book may be used or reproduced in any manner for the purpose of training artificial intelligence technologies or systems. In accordance with Article 4(3) of the DSM Directive 2019/790, penguin Random House expressly reserves this work from the text and data mining exception.

Set in 10.5/16pt Akkurat Std
Typeset by Jouve (UK), Milton Keynes

Printed and bound in Great Britain by Clays Ltd, Elcograf S.p.A.

The authorized representative in the EEA is Penguin Random House Ireland, Morrison Chambers, 32 Nassau Street, Dublin D02 YH68

A CIP catalogue record for this book is available from the British Library

ISBN: 978-0-241-72104-9

Penguin Random House is committed to a sustainable future for our business, our readers and our planet. This book is made from Forest Stewardship Council® certified paper.

Nova Scotia House

1

Let me sort through who I am. Won't take long. Paintings by Jerry. Some books that don't depress me. Furniture is Jerry's, mostly, made by his friends. Two pairs of sneakers, a pair of boots. Two coats – a waterproof and a duffel, back of the door – mine, not his. Jerry's diaries are upstairs, our letters, our paper trail. It is safe.

Stones and stones and stones on shelves. Stones to remember a beach or a time and brought home and they become a stone on the shelf no memory of where it was from or when just stones. I'm so used to the stones I see them and I don't see. Not seeing is more than seeing.

This room is open plan and nothing really and I like that nothing. I come in and there is the kitchen and there is the lounge and there is the door and there is the garden where I grow what I can to eat. It is all the same and one is the other and this is how I like things. I do not want to leave it.

Downstairs is all one room. Upstairs there are rooms but these are not my walls I cannot knock them down so what can I do. Often I sleep down here, in the light, it is better. I don't understand that, sleep in a darkened room. I don't get it I want to see light. I'd sleep in the garden if I could I really would. Things are dying now in the garden I love it. Wait. They're not dying they're dying back.

Almost sunset. The light, we had this light, we have always had this light. They are building those flats, the light will be blocked, that will be it, we will not be able to grow. I don't want to leave I will have to leave I can't leave. Can I stay here why stay here. I don't want to think about it now. I don't want to think. What can I do.

Wait there's more to crop. I missed those tomatoes. End of the season that never ends.

I want a beer and I want that guy to come over and I know he won't come over so why do I bother when I know he won't be coming over. He comes over when he wants to come over and never at my call. It's such a game. Let's look and see if he's on yeah he's on yeah he's ignoring me. The game is the game. What is the game. Can I get out. Do I want to get out. Can I try.

Wait, somebody else. Looks OK. Ha. OK he's alright. Haha OK he knows what he wants. Yeah OK why not. I'll give him the address. Flat 1, Nova Scotia House.

I mean he was alright. Kind of fun. Kind of hot, body gone but who cares. Knew what he was doing. See you around, he said. I'll never see him around. Said he was 41. Yeah right. At least I don't lie. They all lie, everybody lies. I can't lie. I physically can't. Tell a lie and I am red. Always been that way. I never learned how to lie I always give myself away. I'm 48 I'm not going to pretend I'm younger, you can come around you can deal with me being 48 or you can go someplace else.

There's that blue light. The old tower was never meant to

be lit up blue, blue all up in the stairwells, it's all blue now, the blue at night so users can't see their veins. I used to live up there, in that tower that no one has decided is beautiful and so has yet to be colonized, no one wants to live in that tower, no one with money, no one with a choice. Down here it's different, two along went for three quarters of a million. There's me, there's Nasim next door, the family upstairs, four along from them, and that's all that's left. The rest are private. They think they own where they live. Most cases the owner is the bank.

48. Not bad for 48. Some say I look younger. Not many. At school other boys were hot and they knew they were hot and now look at them. I mean I've seen none of them since I've no intention it's another world I would not know them, but when I see photos, sometimes I see photos, I cannot believe I wasted all that time on that kid. What game was I stuck in then, really, what was that game, a game at which I could only lose. What did I put myself through, why. It makes me angry but that anger is long suppressed, angry as a kid, angry for life, suppress it to survive, you pretend it's not there but it's there.

I'm hungry. Use the tomatoes. Pastry first. Enough for one, no wait I can have the rest for lunch tomorrow. Make the pastry, smoosh it together. That was Jerry's word, smoosh. Meant to be a mess. In the fridge a while. It is so warm tonight. Still not needed the heating once.

Everything is everything, Jerry would say, he'd say it with arm actions, his arms spanning a circumference of everything he could span. Food is everything, he'd say. We are the same as it, it is the same as us, we're just molecules, that's all I am, these molecules will soon disperse, they'll find some other purpose, so therefore I'm not me at all, am I really, I'm everything, I'm nothing, same thing.

Jerry was always talking about the trap. He would say that we can avoid the trap. Or we can trap ourselves. They want to trap us, he would say, they want us to rely on them, they profit from us, they pretend to care but what they call food is rot, it will rot you. Grow as much as you can. Buy from good people. It is simple. Live well and be well.

He would say be well even though he was not well, he would say live well and be well until the end.

Fry some onions. Roll out the pastry. Cut these tomatoes in half. Onions on first. Tomatoes on top. A good load of olive oil. Salt. Pepper. In the oven. There are those potatoes left over. Slice them. Fry them. Another beer. It's done.

I am meant to hate myself. I will not play that game. Live alone – I am meant to hate myself. No money – I am meant to hate myself. Lonely – I am meant to hate myself. And then who wins. Everyone and everything that I hate. And so I will not hate myself.

Put on Monk. *Monk's Dream*. Then is now, now is then, don't you see. Our insignificance. I do not know if I make sense but then I do not think we can make sense, there has to be contradiction. What do I know. Wait. I will not hate myself. I will not.

I wake early. Always do. Quiet here. Always has been. All these people and still it is quiet. What is it now. Not yet seven. Still dark. First light will come through the glass on the door, it strikes one of Jerry's paintings, not much else. Once it's up enough it's on the garden pretty much all day long. South-west long length, there used to be space the other side of the fence, until they started to build that block. I wish I could thank whoever first planned this estate, whoever cared, five six seven decades ago, whoever cared to give space to this housing, some people cared. Due at the clinic at eight. Early shift today. On the phones for the first ninety minutes. Then whatever needs to be done. I'll be home by three.

Coffee. The coffee I make is bad coffee but it is the coffee I make. At seven Jerry would put on the news but that was when you could listen to the news. Oats. Is there yoghurt left yes there is. Honey and cinnamon and pumpkin seeds. Wish I could afford almonds, I can't afford almonds. I have a budget I stick to the budget Jerry always stuck to a budget, credit is a trap, he would say, be free.

In is out, it is the same thing. Lucky to have a door that slides open onto this. Why lucky. Should be normal. I'll dig up some spuds later. Pick some greens. Garden is a mess. Should tear it all out, start again. But then what would be lost. This is what time is really. What has been here.

I am a mess and that is that. Why pretend otherwise. Why set myself by someone else's standards. It's all a lie. No standards to judge myself against, no elders, all dead. The ones that survived are broken. Hardened by it. Where is the softness, where is the care. 7.09. Should shower. Might jerk off. Could help.

T-shirt, jeans, too hot in the clinic, always, this is all I need. Fleece for the walk. Still too mild for a coat. I feel so small. What is this. Come on. Let's go. Thursday. Mrs B will be in this morning, no need to see the doctor, she doesn't even pretend any more, she just comes for the gossip. Always. Irene says we're not a drop-in centre, still I'll make

Mrs B a tea. You remind me of my Mike, my boy, that's what Mrs B says. Bet her Mike is also a faggot.

OK, keys. Always pick up Jerry's bunch, four other keys on it that open up I do not know what door. Headphones in. Dusty. 'Breakfast In Bed'.

Out the door. You see the scars. I live in damaged lands. Those old houses over the road – they were not bombed. Small, cramped, never liked them. People pay a fortune now. Or tether themselves to a bank on the promise of a fortune. Not bombed. Bomb scars show now as new estates. Still called new even though they are what five six decades old.

Let's take the back route. Right-hand side of the road, not bombed. Left, bombed. Wait the pub on the corner is old. Not bombed. Wish it had been.

These scars are so normal. They want us to think bombing is normal. Wait, you can get locked into that thinking about some unknown 'they'. Wait, I get locked into that thinking about some unknown 'you'.

Cross the road, but the traffic is not moving anyway, the road may as well be the path, still air, these fumes, all these fumes going into the still air in the garden, that pretence of nature, forget about it. Cut through the park, pretence of nature, what tree ever wanted to be in a line. Woodland area as long as there's nothing the park keeper doesn't want to be in the woodland area. There's the park keeper. Morning. Park keeper nods.

I was brought up on dirt. Drop bread on floor oh it'll be fine. Soil trying to do what it does, probably rubble beneath, not bombing here, rubble from when they built the waterways, used to be a canal here, canal to the power station, long gone, both. Soil on top of that rubble trying to pretend that rubble is natural. What is natural. It smells and I like the smell. Heavy and edible and off.

Wonder if that guy still lives in that apartment. Never see him. Only saw him those few times. In his clothes he was all lies. All a front. When we were naked we barely said anything to each other so what did lies matter. He always came round mine. When he'd first turn up his eyes were always averted, like he couldn't look, but then I'd take his clothes off, that was always the way, I took them off him, and then he would look at me, look and look and when he fucked me he had to be facing me, he had to be able to look.

After we'd hooked up a few times we went to the pub to see what we were in real life, it was my idea, I wanted to see what we were in real life. And when he walked in he said he'd never been here before and I said where do you live and he said, the children's hospital, and that was it. It was only a couple of blocks away. The children's hospital that had been derelict for years. The children's hospital where they filmed hospital dramas for TV when anyone still watched TV, actors acting pain and other actors acting stress and some actors only actors because of their hotness and others for their normalness. Then no one watched TV and the place was derelict again until it was redeveloped as what were called luxury flats which were flats in the wards where children had been in pain and had died. And some people have paid what eight hundred thousand for a tiny share of a ward where children had been in pain and had died. I mean, what does that life mean. He lived there and he'd never been in the pub and in that pub he could barely look at me. Where do you go, I asked him. Not here, he said.

He had one beer and then said he had to go and that was it. And then he blocked me.

Maybe he's looking down now, from the window of his piece of a children's ward. Looking down on this dirt, this soil, this smell. It smells like me, I smell.

There are men ahead they are talking it is demonstrative I tense. They have coffees in their hands, coffees I can't afford. They are talking stood broad loud they make me tense I can't hear them yet wait now I can hear them, nine hundred thousand, one says, the kids love it, what about you.

Go round them quick, quick go round, these masters of that game, don't catch their eye, do not be part of their game. There is always a game I know that. I'm not stupid. Can there be a better game. The smell is strong, my smell. Go out of the park.

More flats, these ones older. Meant to be fancy. Already tatty. Small mean windows. Small mean public garden, not actually public, not gardened. This is the neighbourhood. Shops with all I can't afford now all closed anyway. What is this street meant to be. Still here is the clinic, grills over the windows, signs all over the windows, DO NOT ENTER UNLESS YOU HAVE AN APPOINTMENT; THIS CLINIC IS APPOINTMENT ONLY; ABSOLUTELY NO DROP-INS; CALL BETWEEN 8.30am AND 9.30am FOR AN APPOINT-MENT. Door not open. Knock. Irene opens, disinfectant air. Come in child, she says, as always.

OK that's all done. Mrs B was only in for an hour, Irene only told me off twice, only two patients had a go, one slapped the glass between us and them, it's normal, it's fine, I can't make it better, I can only say what they don't want to hear in a nice way. How nice, I'm complicit.

Got some bulbs to put in. Wild garlic. Will spread everywhere. Alliums for show. So much crammed in, yet I cram in more.

This is how I met Jerry. Yes dear, he said, shove them in, any hole is a goal.

No one had called me dear before. I was a student, had come to the city thinking I'd find what I wanted to find without knowing what I wanted to find and I couldn't find it. I'd done stuff before I'd been with guys I'd done whatever but I had never found what I wanted to find. And then I found it.

That was it. I met Jerry. That set the next four years. The small and the vast. Everything mattered, always. Everything everyday. I said to him once that before him I'd never found it and he said yes dear but you see we're all already dead. Or dying. Nearly four years with Jerry. Died twenty-four years ago.

I met him at a neighbourhood action. Council had made a park then had neglected the park. The council had no interest, no budget so no interest, took no responsibility, no idea what responsibility should mean, they failed at society, or at least at a society that helped each other, that cared.

It was endemic, the lack of care. It was in everything. How had it happened, why, how could it carry on, how could it only get worse.

I was in my second year. Hated college. Hated my course. Hated my first year halls. Thought I'd made a friend then we flatshared then I knew we were not friends. Flat was on the ninth floor of Newfoundland Point, same estate as this place, now it's one of the blue light towers. I did everything I could to get out. Posters were in the stairwell.

VOLUNTEERS WANTED: RECLAIM CARPENTER PARK
NO EXPERIENCE NEEDED
DIGGING * PLANTING * SWEEPING * MENDING

My flatmate I hated said who gives a fuck. I didn't tell him I was going. Colder then. Preparing for real winter. That day raw. Four others volunteered. Jerry one of them.

Linda look I found these. Dumped on the flower market.

Jerry had a string bag in his hand. Black tulips, he said, and he looked at me, and he smiled that smile, the first time he smiled that smile at me. Fancy helping, he said.

It was better than sweeping. He gave me a trowel. Dig twice the height of the bulb, Jerry said. You know which way up right. Bet you know your tops from your bottoms.

I had no idea.

We dug and we planted and for the first time I felt clear around me. I felt possibilities. A hundred bulbs in the bag. Spaced them out. Soil back over them. It looked like nothing but we knew it was there.

I told him I hated my flatmate. He said why and so I told him why. What a bitch, he said about my flatmate, and I had never heard a man call another man a bitch. Pay him no mind, Jerry said, he is irrelevant.

He was irrelevant! I remember thinking, he is irrelevant! I remember thinking, this guy knows me already more than my friend who's not a friend. I remember thinking, I hate my friends. I was always thinking, those were friends only because we were forced together through school, through college, kids forced together, forced to have friends, I hated that hierarchy, hated the acquiescence, sure that's not how I understood it then, that's how I see it now, adult word but that's how it felt, I remember the feeling, the feeling of being trapped and knowing I was being trapped and having no choice but being trapped, that flatness, that lack of possibility, all I wanted was possibility, that's all I wanted. We planted the bulbs.

Jerry then was beyond my understanding of age. He was old but different old. I was what 19. Jerry was not just old he was *old*, a sunkenness. He asked how old I was and I told him and I asked how old he was and he said 45.

I had no idea.

We formed a committee that day, these old people and me, the Carpenter Park Collective. Someone had a camera, there's a photo, Jerry, Me, Linda, that day in front of the black tulip bed, just soil, no tulips. I have it somewhere. I used to hate it. Me gawky and awkward, smiling like it was my first smile, a smile that hurt. Now I can see that I was gawky and awkward and it was my first smile and really it's all OK. That is who you are, I hope that is who I am.

I sometimes feel I cannot I really cannot and I have to make myself try. I feel it now, I cannot. It's such a small thing, these bulbs, I tense up like I cannot. Get them in the earth, I know I will do it, still I tense. Some of these bulbs must have spread from ones Jerry planted. Snowdrops, bluebells. So long since his hands were in this earth, it's still his garden, it's also mine, this is no memorial, don't keep it the same, Jerry said, he hated that, it's a garden, he said, garden it. Do you want your ashes spread here I asked him. Don't you dare, he said, I've haunted you enough.

He went in the river.

That day when we first met, we went for a walk. We'd finished planting the bulbs, had tidied up. He said, do you feel like walking while we still have light. He said, I want to see the river, while I can still see. And so we gave the tools back to Linda, she kept them in her shed.

And then Jerry said, Let's walk shall we. Jerry said it and we walked, and from then our life was walking and I have walked ever since. Twenty-eight years I have kept walking. He should still be alive now he should still be with me we should still be walking.

We walked south out of the park. I had lived in that tower for months, but until then I had not gone south of that street, had not gone further than its corner shop, had not diverged from the little I thought I knew.

Let's go through the city, he said, it's so miserable.

Jerry's stride made him be somewhere before he was there. Mine was hesitant. I lingered. I linger.

I should walk there now. Come on. Stop doing bulbs. If you're going to remember, then remember. Take the same path.

Jerry said, I'm from the edges. If you are born on the edges you should live on the edges. You should never assimilate.

Three houses clung to each other, none other around them. Across the road new housing that was no longer new, boarded up. There was rubbish in the driveway, the rubbish in bags, spilling out of bags, and also what could not fit into bags, a sofa, pram, ironing board, a sink. Next door in the driveway a car burnt out.

It was this one right? The house is still here, now someone lives here, an attempt at a life, the three houses clinging are still there, still clinging, a new build next to them, and another new build, the houses that still cling to each other now disappear, no one cares.

I love this barren land, said Jerry. We had turned onto a road that would have been an artery if anyone wanted to use it, the road broad and no one on it, a worker's café with no workers in it, maybe they were there at dawn, maybe they were never there. We crossed the road, looking though there was no need to look. The other side was pavement and chain fence and then behind it scrub, angry wild free plants, ugliness on display, the edge of the city heralded by ugliness, that is what I remember thinking, ugliness and danger, I did not feel safe, Jerry stopped at the fence and put his fingers through the fence and said, how beautiful.

I could not see that it was beautiful and it was not until we had walked this walk often and seen change and seen season and individual plants that I stopped seeing wild ugliness and I saw it as beautiful.

Those asters, said Jerry, I didn't know what an aster was, he pointed into the ugly mass, at a plant, its flowers as dots aggressive with life. Show me an aster in a flower bed and I am so bored, he said, an aster in barren land makes me wild.

I've never grown asters in our flower bed since.

That barren land stretched blocks, barren land from the train tracks that ran above it and beneath it, two levels of train tracks, one track escaping out of the city, one skirting its border, barren land either side, barren land that no one wanted, why would anyone want that land, what would anyone do with it.

Now the barren land is gone. Now there are flats and flats and flats piled awkward high, piles of flats precarious blocking the light all around, the flats are like what lowest price eight hundred thousand for what a studio which is basically a cupboard north facing no light out onto nothing, and now no one wants these flats anyway, no one in the flats, but the flats remain, like the flats are more important than the people, the people below, the people overshadowed.

This is the border, said Jerry, we had started walking again, had walked under the bridge. It is magic, can you feel its tension.

I think I said something like it's so horrible here or it feels so lonely here or it's so desolate or it's so unloved or maybe I said these things on other walks other times we walked over the border I can't remember.

That's the tension, he said, to whatever it was I said, he probably said it all the other times to all the other things I said, on other walks, over the years, while he could still walk, that is what I love, I love this reality, before that horror.

Under the bridge. Other side boarded up, posters once on it but the posters now torn, a gate, padlocked, the parties are down there, said Jerry. We should go sometime.

I did not know what to say. Was he asking me on a date. I'd slept with guys but no one had asked me out on a date before. I'd not let anyone. I did not say anything, did not know what to say.

Jerry said, it's like a shoreline. We were on the edge of the city, tight crammed row washed up, four storeys tight crammed, what would have been shops boarded up, a pub not a pub for some long time, what would have been offices above, warrens, offices for those who wanted a city address but couldn't afford the city, this was near enough. Now the pub that is no longer a pub is still there, its façade, the rest of the building gutted, the façade of the pub now the entrance for what has been shoved behind and above it, another precarious pile of flats, this pile what fifty flats high, fifty flats piled on top of each other, no one in the flats, no one cares.

No one wants us here, said Jerry. The city is not meant for us. As he said it, he strengthened his stride into that city. I remember his purpose, he always had purpose.

It was a dank land, I did not understand it, could not comprehend its roads, its paths, its meaning, where it went, it is still that way to me now, I do not understand it, the city does not want me to understand it, that is not its purpose, the city is there to make money for others, I do not make money, nor did Jerry, we were everything it is not, we were proud of it, I am proud of it. He taught me to walk where we were not wanted.

That first walk we crossed into the city, the difference was decay. Before we crossed into the city everywhere was tatty, unkempt. In the city the dankness was part of the order, the greyness was desired, it was meant to repel, we do not want to interest you, go away. We went on.

There was no one then. There is no one now. What can I remember, what does the present wipe out. These towers here now, they pretend to have always been here, they pretend permanence, what was before them, but there were towers then, many less than now, towers that were never friends, never acknowledge each other's presence, unknown to each other, they will never meld.

We walked the grey streets. What are these buildings, attempts at grandeur, grandeur for who, who is then denied, most of us. It's all so old, I remember saying. Jerry said, is it old, what is old, this is not old, it is a lie.

That greyness is still here, still trying to be old. Jerry said, look at those poor dears, he pointed up, a building of grandeur had attempted further grandeur by trimming its roof with sculptures, men with swords, women draped, attempting grandeur except they were soot black and netted, each one trapped in net, forlorn, prey abandoned, humiliated for how long, decades, netted then, still netted now, their shame relentless. How bleak, netted humans high and dry, soiled, this is grandeur.

Let's cut down here, said Jerry, he took a side street, and I remember our bodies banging into each other, as if first a test to see if our bodies wanted to be together, then again, our bodies touching when they could, that's how it happened, that's how we happened, through our bodies, our bodies told us. Little daylight down the side street, just wide enough for a car, but there were no cars, we walked down the middle of the street, bodies banging, no need to acknowledge it, no need to say a word, we knew, the side street fed into another alley, then another, I was lost, downhill, round a corner, buildings more intense, a sudden slope like it was all about to fall.

Not far, said Jerry. Over a main road with no one on it, cut down alongside the beginning of a railway bridge, at the end steps that went up to nowhere down, and here she is, said Jerry.

We were at the river. Come up here, it goes nowhere, said Jerry, steep steps up to a platform, the platform out over the water, it was low tide, I had not known a river could have tides, oh yes she pulls it in, she pushes it out, said Jerry. He pointed to the water, it was pulling in two directions at once, the flow of the river, its tidal retreat, across the river buildings that no one knows because no one needs to know them, what were wharfs, now maybe homes, now maybe offices, no one knows.

No one comes here, said Jerry, I always come here and there is never anyone here.

As he said it, someone walked by, he saw them and smiled, he meant what he said, no one meant no one, they were no one, he was no one, I was no one.

How strange to be taken to desolation, abandonment, the river not caring, continuing with its pull, down below what would you call it, a beach, doesn't a beach mean beauty, it was an abandonment, rubble revealed by low tide, the rubble held in by timbers, a created beach, now abandoned, if the river had its way the beach would be long gone, the rubble would be pulled away, deposited elsewhere, this bank on the top of a curve, here the current unrelenting, taking what it can, the current knows what it wants to do, the rubble is still there now, still held in by timber, maybe the timber is more rotted, who knows, further along two pylons, a pole, in the water, no reason, abandoned. Whatever their purpose before, something maritime, now just abandoned, I asked Jerry questions, he told me what he knew and what he presumed, no distinction between the two, water vaguely clean to about an inch depth, then it gave up.

    Look the other way and the bridge is a block, blocks what is known of the city, what are called landmarks, marking the land for those who will never visit the land, or for those who visit the land briefly, for one time, the few who are allowed in, those who live long-term often blind to these markers of land, the bridge blocks them anyway, it is like they are eradicated, wiped out, that land is no longer marked.

    There was a ladder down from the platform, spindly, ambivalent. Someone was on the rubble down below, looking through the rubble, picking rubble up, tossing it back, sometimes putting it in a bag, they were alone, down there outside of time, outside of this realm. I said, how do we get down, Jerry said, this way.

    He led me to more steps up the river wall, this time with steps down the other side, down to the abandoned realm, a barge on the abandonment tethered to the right, as if the barge had never been used, only abandoned, timbers fallen in the rubble, compounded by the rubble, some sense of line in the rubble, the line going nowhere.

    The walls of the river were patched, sometimes metal sheets, sometimes brick, sometimes smeared with concrete, patched up then patched again, the city held back, it all just wants to fall, the same now, the same then, am I talking about now, am I talking about then, no difference, Jerry is not here, do not believe in magical thinking, he is gone, that is it.

    These river walls, is this how all buildings would be if

they were out of sight, patched then patched again, no care, these walls that hold in the river, fundamental and unloved, we walked under the bridge, the pillars holding up the bridge weirdly grand, no reason for the grandeur, no one sees them, the bridge itself ugly, no attempt at show, yet down here, rows of columns, tightly packed in, taking the weight of the trains above, the passengers, if there were any, the columns fluted, as if they were made by the people who occupied this land two thousand years ago, here now rows and rows of these fluted columns that no one can see, this expanse across the water, water dripping from the bridge, then I had never taken a train from that station, still have not to this day, no clue where its trains go, if they go anywhere.

    There is someone on the rubble today, same place as the person then, same process, picking up whatever is there, throwing it back, putting some bits in a bag, bones, shells, crockery, glass, we were walking on bones, shells, crockery, glass, if the person was aware of me they must have looked up without moving, then and now, I remember their isolation then, their commitment, this existence outside of time, I wanted that same existence, I try for that same existence.

    Timbers on the river wall trying to hold back the city, some still vertical, others come undone and spun, spun by the tide, now pointing at angles, as if telling time, trying to impose time on this land out of time, one at 18 minutes past the hour, the other at 42. We walked to the edge of what was abandoned, timber worn away at the end, water coming where it shouldn't, we stood looking at the pylons, back then there was nothing of note on the skyline behind, south of the river then not land that was cared about, a veil drawn, now a pointed tower has been built near the river on the south, a tower that looks like it doesn't exist, that it isn't really there, pointless height, a boast that impresses no one, the abandoned pylon in the water and the pointed tower behind both as useless as each other.

How often do you come here, I asked Jerry, as often as I can, he said, and we would come here often. This is my first time back in years. Don't dwell, Jerry would say, don't hold on to what is gone, nostalgia is death, the past is boring, what about now.

But then Jerry was always telling me about the past, using the past to look forwards, not dwelling in the past, learning from the past, no desire to repeat the past, the desire to make something new. He was always telling me something, always trying to get me to understand, even if he didn't understand it himself, it was urgent for him, was it always urgent, was he always urgent or was it that this was all he had left.

It was getting dark on that first day, that first walk, what had I been taught before, what everyone had been taught, learning by rote, learning that told me nothing except I did not want to be that way, to live like them, I did not want to live how I was being taught to live, subservient, straight. That day I remember the smile on my face, why are you smiling, he said, it's miserable. Jerry was smiling too, I did not know what to say and I knew that it did not matter that I did not know what to say. I am not meant to know what to say I can just show it. So much time wasted before, so much time wasted not knowing what to say, so much time wasted not showing it, clamped up, this is repression, the repression of thinking that words are the only way out, they are not, the way out is with the body.

By this water I smiled. Thank you, I said to Jerry. What for, he said. Bringing me here, I said. What to this fucking dump, he said, he smiled. The cold is getting to my bones, Jerry said, fancy getting the bus.

Up the steps, up the road, out.

Don't want to go home yet. Why do I not come here more. Water is so placid. Nearly the turning point, the pull will start again soon. What is still here from then, what remains. Loose bones, constant circulation, these bones will be back in the water when the tide comes in again, back in circulation, to be dropped somewhere else, picked up, dropped, eventually they must rot, surely, yet these bones are so old.

Jerry sparked me. Before Jerry I was asleep. People would say you two were meant to be together. Jerry has been gone twenty-four years now, if we were meant to be together he would be here. We were not meant to be. Nothing was meant to be. We just were, why lie, why does anyone need these words.

Getting dark. What am I doing here. Back up the steps, back up to presumed order, I'll come here again soon, I promise, who am I promising.

Wait I don't want to go. Go back to where Jerry took me first. Lean on the wall, look over. Water starting to pull. Stillness so fleeting. Someone else on the path, hi-vis. Security guard. Slow pacing in front of the building one along. The guard is looking at me. Am I not meant to be here. What are my rights. What is this land. It looks public, is it public.

Guard hesitates. Isn't coming closer. Maybe the guard can't leave the territory in front of the building, a non-delineated delineated space, the guard is still looking at me, am I trouble, someone is coming, blue shirt, no tie, trousers, sneakers, a backpack, I am staring don't realize I am staring he is looking at me now he is staring his air in my air too close, you OK mate, he is smiling, still walking but slow, like he could keep going but he could also stop, I cannot say words, try to stumble out a word, an acknowledgement, but there are no words, is he coming on to me, all this happens in nanoseconds, I have no clue. I do not respond, am flummoxed, maybe I am afraid, to respond would be to open myself up, I still cannot open myself up. He goes by, I look back, he does not look back, too late, who is the one with the problem.

2

Day to myself. Will I see anyone. Will I see anyone. Don't care. Sounds rude, it's not rude, it's not antisocial, I don't need to see anyone.

Cut back the hellebore leaves. So brutal. Right down to the bottom. Jerry would say pretend it's dead. They are last year's leaves, they've done their work, they still want to hang around, if I let them hang around there'll be less flowers, I cut the leaves to force it to flower, gardening is a trick, it is gruesome.

Some of these hellebores were planted with Jerry, I planted them, Jerry told me what to do, by then he was too weak. His mind was just as brutal. Pretend it's dead.

When they were planted the hellebores were pretty much on their own for months, nothing much else flowering, everything else pretending it was dead, waiting for the light to return, now it's all early, everything thinks it's spring, everything trying its hand in winter, wait it's not even winter yet, it is autumn.

Message from Nasim. In my phone as Nasim 2 Nova Scotia. She can't get an answer from the owners of number 5, number 6, number 8, number 10. Owners of number 9 say they don't care, and so right now there's no majority there's no consensus they can keep saying to us that they have majority approval even though that majority is people in the whole area, not the estate, the question so vague that most would say yes: do you agree there should be more housing in this area? 76% said yes, I said yes, and so now they say they have permission to build that tower into that space where there should be no tower. Space was part of the design of the estate, space was an ideal of living, it is now there for exploitation, it is now there for profit, we are here to lose.

I will lose. Nasim will lose. The tower will block my light. Completely. It will block Nasim's light. We both grow as much food as we can. We can't afford otherwise. Nasim feeds a family of six. If she has no light, nothing will grow.

Nasim is fighting, I am fighting, we don't own our places, we have no rights, we have no clout, what do they care, they do not want us to live. I mean it they just want us to consume, I will not just consume I want to live. Most of the flats are absentee landlords most don't care, most of the gardens left overgrown, dumping grounds, the odd garden prettified for a minute then the tenants get bored and leave it and the prettification sours and they spend their lives looking out on what they gave up.

Dig up a celeriac. It's huge. Will do me good for the week. Some cabbage to make kraut. Beans are soaking. Will cook them soon. Five weeks to the shortest day and still OK in just a sweater. Still OK. It is not OK.

This will be my last year of winter light. Make the most of what I have while I have it. Is that accepting defeat. The council has played us for fools, the council that planned this estate doesn't exist any more, disbanded not long after the estate was finished, the new council never liked the estate, never cared, never put into action any visionary plans, yes the estate was visionary, they left it to ruin, did not care, soon it was ruined, squalid, a self-fulfilling prophecy, nightmare estate, no-go zone, Jerry got this flat because it was a no-go zone, at the time the council saw the no-go flats as a solution for those evicted from squats, only faggots would want them, Jerry would say.

    What does new mean. The estate is fifty years old. Cook the beans, put it on, leave it, keep an eye.

    No one wanted to live here, that's how we got the flat in the tower, in my second year, no one else wanted it, we could afford it, me and my friend, my ex-friend. Council didn't care, council only started to care when money started coming, when people who'd had their backs to us suddenly turned around, suddenly wanted to live here, suddenly the council found the money to do the flats up, barely did them up, did the minimum, and then did all they could to exploit the estate, this bankrupt council, exploit what had been visionary, and so they sold off that space, space that had been for everyone suddenly for none of us, sold, no mention to us, no sign of plans until it was already sold, decision already made, we were always on the backfoot, played for fools, who am I, what am I, why should they care anyway, they don't care.

    Mushy light. What am I meant to be doing now. Day off. Off from what. Door is open. No need for heating yet. Mushy city. Record is finished and I never even heard what it played. Put it on again. Sly Stone. *There's a Riot Goin' On*. Got it when I was a kid. Not mushy then. Dank then.

    Do not live by their schedule do not be a robot do not let

time be imposed upon you they are using you. Jerry would say this and he was only talking about television, I wanted a television, he would not let me get a television, I hated him for not letting me get a television, I've not had a television since.

I'd want one for those days we'd lie on the sofa recovering, still drunk, me still out of my mind, I wanted a television, Jerry would not let me get a television.

That first weekend. Jerry rang me. Those parties I was telling you about, dear, under the arches. There's one this weekend, fancy coming?

I'd got no other plans, didn't want to stay in, Jerry said come down to his place first, 9pm Saturday, he said do you want my address? Number 1 Nova Scotia House.

That Saturday I came here. I'd not been to this bit of the estate before. Hard, harsh, low. I knocked, Jerry opened, you came, wonderful. Others were here, Gareth, someone else, Sam? Fiona. Older. Older as in they knew what they were doing. Or looked as if they knew what they were doing. Had learned how to look like they knew what they were doing. They were warm and they were amused and they were welcoming and they were hesitant. Jerry was Jerry. I had no clue. What was this world. Come look at the garden, he said, and then, these are my paintings, and then, make yourself at home.

There was space on the sofa by Gareth, I took it, I tried not to feel under threat. Gareth asked me questions.

Where did you meet Jerry? Volunteering. What do you do? I'm at college. How old are you? 19.

Jerry gave me vodka. It helped. Gareth had finished with me, Gareth joined in with whatever Fiona and the other guy were saying. Time passed. I was in the circle and not in the circle. I followed as well as I could. Most was gossip. I laughed when they laughed. No one really talked to me and I felt stupid and I felt alive.

We were there for ever. What do you do, I said to Fiona. PhD in architecture, she said. What do you study, I said. Impossible buildings, she said. Have you built anything, I said. No, she said. Leaving soon, she said, west coast.

I could form no bond I did not yet know how. When we left, the other guy said to Jerry, one of your waifs and strays, and Jerry said, I have an open-door policy. Smiled at me as he said it. We set off, Jerry striding ahead, I was by his side. You OK, he said, and then, they like you.

We took the same path, rowdier and more silent, walked through bursts of rowdiness then streets with no one, nowhere, no one wanted to come here, no one saw this as pleasure, so far from anything that seemed like pleasure. The party's run by my friend from when we squatted, said Jerry, he was part of a collective, they ran parties, only him left, and me, the rest are dead.

The border was broad, unloved, no one wanted to cross into our world, no one wanted us part of theirs. Few lights picked out the border, the streetlights dim or broken, no need for lights anyway, no one there. But then there were people. A queue. Back to where we had stood the other day, looking into the scrub, the caged wild, the asters still there in their darkness.

Gareth said can't we jump the queue and Jerry said he would never jump the queue, that is not how it should be. Fiona said will we get in and Jerry said, we'll be OK.

I did not think we would be OK, I did not think we would

get in, we were too late, there'll only be space for them, not for me, they'll leave me outside, I didn't deserve it, no one cared, the usual.

Queue took for ever, for ever meaning what, an hour? For ever. It moved. The people in front of us jovial, Gareth being vile about them to Jerry, to me, being vile to pass time. Finally we got there. The gate that had been locked was open. A table, doorperson, two guards. Jerry said his name and he said plus four, the doorperson said, of course Jerry, happy to see you. Stamp on our wrist, a coiled snake, guards patted us down but didn't care really, we were through.

Suddenly no people, or barely any people at least, a long covered passage running alongside the bridge, curving off in the distance, endless bridge arches leading off to where vision doesn't work, unexpected perspective, long dark hall, rubble and dust floor, it stank, no one ever intended anything to be under here, just concrete columns, columns lined up, off into the unseen, this dark promenade, there were others in front of us, some coming from behind running, we could not hear it and then we heard it.

People more people then an arch, noise like I had not known it, a hard wall, relentless, so many bodies, light mostly red, smoke steaming from bodies, smoke from cigarettes, chemical smoke in the air, Jerry came close grinning maniacal, in my ear he said, follow me, and Jerry took my hand. He pulled me through those who did not want to relent, there was no way through, he found a way through. We made it to the front there was nowhere to go but Jerry kept pulling, Jerry went to the railings and went to the side of the railings and we were out the other side. I should not have been there what was I doing there, Jerry still held my hand, pulled me to some people, hugged them each in turn, introduced me to them each, I couldn't hear, I smiled, it was everything, I was behind the rail, near the DJ, behind the line. This is Dave, Jerry said, it was Dave's party. I just smiled, I was too shy, I didn't yet know how to be, didn't yet know what to say, didn't yet know it was OK to be. They talked, I didn't try to join, I looked into the crowd, I wanted to be in the crowd, I was looking at them, some of them seeing me, most not, most didn't care, I started dancing next to Jerry, it was unreal, it was all I wanted, this world, I hadn't known how to find it, Jerry brought me to the world I wanted.

 Jerry passed me a beer, I said I wanted to go into the crowd, was that OK, I could stay there with him if he wanted. He said, I'll be here, he said, if you want to leave let me know, I said, I don't ever want to leave.

 I didn't know who was playing the records I didn't care I loved it I loved them I loved it. Bought a pill from someone and that was it. I remember everything I remember nothing, everything mattered, nothing mattered, made out with some guy, he was a mess, I was a mess, then he was gone, or had I gone? Don't remember. I was at the back, at the side, all over. I was down the front again, Jerry still there, he smiled and nodded, smile always, he was watching and smiling, his contentment was everything, I loved him. Jerry handed a beer across the railing, bottle of water too, this was real, I remember thinking, whatever it was, I didn't know what it was, this was real. Me at the front, Jerry nearby, Jerry never came out onto the floor, he had no need, always stayed by the speaker, then sat on the speaker, grin intent, he was watching I was watching, this was real.

 Time looped. Vague daylight into the arch, everything

continued, less people but it continued, Jerry still there, I was exhausted, bored, riveted, free. I wanted it to end and I wanted to stay for ever. It's how I felt then, it's how I feel now. I was alone and not alone. It finished when it finished. It made sense. We had seemed a mass but when it was finished we dissipated quick, no more we. Jerry, Gareth still there, not the other guy, not Fiona, Jerry said, fancy coming back to mine.

The world was funny. Buses were funny. Rubbish was funny. Crossing the road was funny. Buying vodka from a shop that shouldn't sell us vodka was funny. It was nine in the morning or something. I hated the neighbourhood. It was nothing like where I thought I would be. I was scared. The neighbourhood was funny. We got to his door. I didn't leave.

Haven't been out like that for a long while. Comedown doesn't suit me. My head got into a bad place for a while. Wasn't worth it. But wait, I could do it now. Go out. Don't need to take anything. What time is it, nine. Come on.

Message Dave. Can he put my name on the door. He's not seen the message he's seen the message he's replying to the message. Sure he says, heart, thumbs up.

Do I smell, no. Put on those jeans, that T-shirt, that shirt. Don't do it up. OK we're good. Fleece over the top. Wait check no one has messaged. No one has messaged, they won't message, don't wait for them to message, don't wait.

Walk to the tube, get on the tube, no one else on the tube. Impatient. Some guy gets on the tube, sits opposite me, he sits opposite but two away, that'll do. His legs spread. Stare at him then not stare. Doesn't look back. Stare at him then not stare. Stare. Doesn't look back. Waggles his legs, widens them then closes them then widens them. Is that a sign. Hand over his crotch is he grabbing it is he hard. Stare at him stare at his crotch, waggle my leg, he waggles his leg, it is on. He gets out his phone, he looks at his phone, don't look at your phone look at me, he puts his phone in his pocket he looks at his fingernails, he crosses his legs, it is not on.

Impatient. Almost there. No queue. Am I too early is anyone there I bet it's a washout I should have stayed home.

In the door. Dark, dank, it stinks, I'm home. OK there are people here, OK it's good, OK it's fun, OK here we go, nice arse, who is he, oh fuck it's him not him no, go round the other side, twenty-three seconds here and already avoid avoid avoid. Who is playing records oh it's Luke, wave, has he seen me, he's waved, hello!

Get a beer. Alright trouble, barman says. Some old drama playing on the screens, screens everywhere, sound off, old drama, soap opera, actors are screeching at each other, pulling hair, wigs must be fixed tight. Love this bullshit, barman says. Saw it when it came out, I say to him.
He can't hear me. Beckon him closer. Say it into his ear. I saw it when it came out. Alright grandma, he says.

That guy over there, always in here, must be as old as Jerry would have been now. In his seventies. Jerry would have loved it here. Nod to him. Doesn't nod back. Doesn't look. Doesn't need to look. Screeching children running calamity. Can't believe their luck, this world in which they get to screech and be calamitous. Let's play who's not been to bed. Screeching children yes, they've been to bed, their clothes are too clean, their screeching too coherent. That pack by the pool table, they have not been to bed. The state of them. Him with his jeans half down staggering around, that guy holding him up, sunglasses on inside, another guy trackpants top off skin no sign of nutrients, world of his own is he dancing is he in a world of his own is he both? Another guy bangs into him they laugh the other guy hands him something security guard not too far away they would be out if they were caught they don't care world of their own, definitely not been to bed, one night up, two? Two other guys making out locked on tops off jeans not wanting to stay up belts holding them up jeans almost off their hips belts barely hanging on like they could give up. The two guys skinny, maybe no nutrients put in their body all weekend, maybe no nutrients because they deprive themselves of nutrients, but both had slight bellies, maybe from the beer they've poured into themselves all weekend, maybe their bodies protesting at the lack of nutrients, distended, they don't care, why should they care? Definitely not been to bed.

Patrick's over there, he's smiling, saluting, smile back, maybe I'll speak with him later, he's not come here to speak with me, he's come here to hook up, let him get on with it, let him hunt around, maybe we'll dance near each other later, maybe we'll talk, maybe. Grace, now Loleatta, now Evelyn, now Yvonne, now Diana. Records I recognize and many I don't, I love that I do and I love that I don't.

Filling up, more arriving, what time is it, still early, what was this pub before, who came here, what was their life, when did it become queer, it's so grand, the squalor, central bar, people all round, booths, dancefloor, maybe it was always a place of pleasure, some guy told me once it used to be all vinegar factories round here, when vinegar was valuable. Apt. Sour queens. How many of those sour queens were queer, how did queers congregate, how did they gather. Here I have come alone and it is my choice I don't need friends I don't need their shit I'm sorry. It is gorgeous here it is so sophisticated I mean it the allowance the release. The sex. The honesty. The abandon.

Who's that guy over there, that face that flesh that presence, that awkwardness, I like him, where are his bones from how did he become that way, what mother what grandmother what father what grandfather, back and beyond, how did all that come to be him, has he seen me has he seen me keep looking has he seen me he's seen me. He looks away.

How old is he, thirties maybe, temples showing a bit, flesh under the chin, he's unsharpened, fleshy flesh, stubbled, he's talking with some guy they're laughing are they together no I don't think they're together they're starting to dance they're still at the bar and they're starting to dance, shirt open, he's nice and hairy, fleshy and doesn't care. 'Right In The Socket'. His friend has a little bottle, he sniffs it, hands it to the guy, he stops dancing, holds it under his nose, breathes it in deep, other nostril, holds it there long, lifts his head up mouth wide eyes to the ceiling and beyond and then he laughs and then he huddles with the other guy, fuck they're together, he's holding the other guy's shoulders, they are head to head, dancing, 'Pick Me Up I'll Dance', wait he's laughing again, they grab each other, hold each other, release, they are released, he is looking at me he is looking how is he looking does he understand does he know.

The other guy whispers in his ear and the guy nods and

he turns the other guy round and then they head to the floor, the guy with his hands on the other guy's shoulders, is he going to look is he going to look he does not look. There's now a crowd they have to get through the crowd, drag queens on the platform, off duty, everyone here just for play, I can't see them, OK I see them, OK they're going deep on the floor, OK I'll go there soon. Not now. Soon.

Who is here alone who is with others. Most here with others, most in groups, maybe they came alone and found friends here, maybe it was a week-long plan, maybe they've been out Friday night Saturday night all day Sunday, now they're here, the natural choice, more than they could ever imagine, where have they pushed themselves to, what is their internal logic telling them, what have they let fall away, who have they not gone home to, who have they not called, what will be the cost.

Another pint. Some guy next to me is saying something. What? Can't hear him, not interested, don't care. I smile mouth shut looking away, he gets it, he moves away, it's not rude, it's how things work, it works, it's primal, it's elemental.

She's on the screen again, her in that nightie, sat in that baby's crib, eating eggs, screaming for more eggs, all she wants is eggs, she loves eggs. 'In The Evening'. All I want.

This is Jerry's music. He'd say, my formative years, he'd play me the records, eight minutes long, eleven minutes, seventeen minutes, we'd listen to it all, the artistry, the sophistication, the pleasure, the sadness, the yearning, the defiance, the bravery, the experimentation, the lightness, we'd talk about why this music was mocked, why it was misunderstood, why it was parodied, why it was ignored. It was made by queer black geniuses, dear, he'd say, what do you expect.

That's what makes it so potent, he'd say, so alive, it's by the marginalized, this was their outlet, this was a place of expression, they could create their own world, some could, not all, not most, some could escape, for a while, never really free, what they did, what they made, the daring, the power, the eloquence, what they let people feel, what they let me feel.

OK the floor is enough to go out and not be an outlier. Some days I'm OK to be an outlier, to try and make a night happen, to try and make others dance, to try and pretend to enjoy dancing on my own when no one else is dancing, not tonight, not what I need, tonight I need more stealth, move to the edge of the floor, the floor now a mass, the floor well lit, the point is to see people, the point is for others to see you, attraction, rejection, either, the whirl, camaraderie, familiarity, acceptance, open-ended energy, OK I'm dancing, push through, oh fuck spilt beer, sorry, he doesn't care, so awkward, where's some space, OK here, I am so not in it, I am so not part of it, I'm so embarrassed, maybe I should stop dancing, maybe I should move, I'm ruining these people's nights, oh wait, OK he's over there, where is he, can't see him now, be cool, you're in it, it's OK, you've melded with these people, they've accepted you, you're here now, these songs, their reality, that life, we need to have it now, that allowance, that acceptance, is this really what I'm thinking right now, here, yes it is, always overthinking, I love overthinking, think more, always think more. I can't see him, it's OK, a huddle next to me, huddled round a little bottle, they take their turn, I want some, they can sense by how I'm standing I want some, they offer me some, OK breathe it in, breathe it, OK away we go, it's too much   it's too much   shit   no it's OK   ha it's OK   .

Another pint. How many is it now four. Five? And sambuca. Another. I'm a mess. What is it now 2.17. Want to leave no stay, forty minutes left, you can do it, come on do it, make it to the end, go back and dance again, sloppy as fuck , spill more beer oh fuck sorry spill loads so have others the floor so wet so gross wait take off your shirt tie it round your waist beer between your knees spill more oh fuck OK let's go, the mass has thinned inevitable, it's OK, bet they have to work in six hours, they've had enough, they've hooked up, whatever, the mass still exists, still enough, end of the night records now, our reward, 'Was That All It Was', how old is this now what four decades , how irrelevant that time , obsession with time, subservient to it , weapon of those who exploit, who make us consume, need for more need for new , none of it matters what matters is a person and what they do and what they create , sloppy as fuck, come on , keep upright banging into others do they care it's allowed wait he's there   wait he's right here   what's happening   it's like we're dancing in a circle me him three others I don't know does he know them where is his friend ? Look at him he's looking at me wait be cool   look around, she's still on the platform, that queen, all-nighter, that other queen's taken it all off, back in boy drag, vest and track-pants, slight young thing, the wig the heels the aura take up so much space, take them away they're meek, this little presence all that presence inside them , OK look back at him again he's looking at me he's waiting for me to look again   he smiles   we hold eyes   he smiles he looks down like he has to focus on the most important thought in the world.

   'Come To Me' ha OK yes. OK a bit closer, the circle has gone the others becoming part of some other circle bubbles that form then burst   his shirt open now   that hair that flesh   his lower lip wide broad putty   mouth more than a smile   we dance we dance we look we don't look   sip of my pint   he looks   he raises his eyebrows   holds his hand out   he wants some   I give him some. Hands it back   our hands touch as he does so   it's a nano nanosecond longer than it's meant to be   it's not awkward   it's awkward   it's intentional   it's his path it's my path   he's leaning in   he's in my space   he's crossed that line his force I can smell him he's leaning in his shirt is touching me he's saying something, what? Can't hear him, I go close to his ear, can't hear you I say close, my lips touch his ear as I say it I know what I'm doing, his hand round my back to pull me closer he says into my ear, Craig, voice is soft like it doesn't have to try, like there's intimacy already, there is intimacy already, we just created it, a dual act, his lips touch my ear too, he still has his arm round my back, put mine round his lower, pull him closer, his chest against mine, closer he's hard, can he feel I'm hard too he can. He's still by my ear his cheek pulls forward against my cheek stubble against stubble let that friction have its effect, his mouth is on mine, locked, open all, eyes closed, this clarity, he is beautiful, beauty, I cannot believe, yes I can believe, stubble sting open, his hand goes to my butt, grabs it, he can grab it, soften into his hand to let him know he can grab it, he knows what he wants, are we banging into people I don't care my hand down in his back pocket jaw wider jaw cannot get wider he tastes gross I want more, wait I want some air, we uncouple, he takes my hand, that smile, eyes heavy, pulls his jeans up, watch him, watch the jeans get caught on his cock, he sees me watching, he smiles, there is no one else here no one.

All so quick outside of time. Takes out his poppers he has some I have some   pushes me back up against a wall   I let him   takes my hands   pushes them back above my head   holds me there   hard   up against me.

   Mouth on my mouth now mouth closed teeth together grin rictus I am looking at him he at me this now about power and control and I let it be. We are messes fall into each other hold each other up, support relent I do not know why I am laughing. The songs come and they come, 'Take Me Home', 'Last Dance', there is everyone there is no one he is all that matters and then it is over.

   Music stops lights on brutal air changes, the space the music took up in the room deflated, the charge of the humans who activated the room, gone. We are wrecks, now we can't hide it, we are also we, that is clear, unless one of us breaks the we, or the other, it's in our power, he comes to me and his mouth is on mine again and then he says you're coming with me right. I just raise my eyebrows yes. Feet foggy. Mild out. His arm round me pressing sweat into sweat. Two minutes, he says, already ordered a car, grateful someone else is organized, how old are you, he says, voice less soft, maybe it's just less soft because it's not by my ear, maybe this is just how he is when he's doing admin, maybe this is just how he is. 48, I say.

   Oh, he says.

how old are you, I say.

He says, 36.

Car comes we get in legs spread his hand on my thigh my hand on his hand. I say to him, what happened to your friend, he says, he got thrown out. He is looking out the window he says nothing else. I say, is he OK, he says, he's always OK.

Not this way, he says loud, then he says nothing. He's speaking at the driver. Then he says, idiot.

Look in the driver's mirror the driver makes eye contact with me we hold eye contact I try and let him know this is not me. The driver looks at me and looks at me and looks away, I don't know where we are going I don't know where we are. We are south of the river I do not know my way. He has my hand he takes my hand he puts it on his crotch, it's hard, I want it.

You fucking missed it, the guy says. Driver pulls up jolts stop, the driver says, should I reverse, tries to see out the back, he can't see out the back. Go round the corner says the guy whose crotch my hand is on, wait what is his name again, fuck, I can't remember, fuck. We are turning the corner, suddenly we're on the road up to a bridge, bridge all lit up pretending to be a castle it's not a castle. Just here, says whoever he is. Car stops cars behind beep so much aggression. He opens the door, whoever he is, he says, maybe learn to fucking drive, he gets out, he's shut the door already, the driver is looking round at me, I say, sorry, I say, thank you, the driver says, arsehole.

River wind. The guy is on the pavement. Bridge is old but not as old as it looks it's a lie. New builds abrupt by pavement crammed in, this is us, he says, takes my hand, are we going to the river, sit by the river, we'll see the river, he lives looking at the river, whoever he is, pulls me down an alley between the new builds. Convenience store on the ground floor that sells barely anything not wrapped in plastic and people live their life from it, no choice everything wrapped in plastic it's called convenience. Office entry lobby wait he's taking out an entry card we're going into an office he's holding the card to a sensor there is a beep there is another beep he pushes open the door to the office, he says, welcome home.

In the office lobby there's a desk there's a security guard he looks at us he says nothing the guy pulls me to the lift we're at the lifts I am laughing he says, what's funny.

He looks at me looks at the lift number it's at 4 it's at 3 I can no longer smell him I can only smell cleaning chemicals or maybe it's the chemical scent to cover up the cleaning chemicals they're both the same.

Lift door open, go in, he gets in, I fall on him he pushes me away, he says, they're watching, he looks up top corner raises his eyebrows I can't see anything what am I doing here. Chemical idea of cleanliness overpowering what have I done with my nose. His hands are in his pockets he wants me to look he is hard he wants me to see he is hard I can barely stand. In a moving box with no window can you tell if you are going up down left right backwards forwards. Lift is slowing it stops no jerk. He goes first what is his name, turns left chemical smell corridor, carpet wipe clean, his size his heft his breadth broad shoulders weighted steps. Gets to a door, anodyne, look on his face of wait-until-you-see, top teeth biting bottom lip rictus grin. Impressed with himself. He opens the door, door swooshes like a door trying to convince itself it's a special door and failing. We go in, it closes, it clicks.

It's like a showroom of an apartment. It's like rendered images on the side of construction sites meant to make you think anything the contractor was building had value, that they were adding anything to a community, the word is aspiration, nothing quite right in the rendered image, the ceiling a little too low, the couch too big, couch that looks like it's never been sat on, art on the wall that never meant anything to anyone, maybe it never even existed, just a rendering, a dumb indoor plant too dumb to know it's indoors, books that have never been read, maybe they were never meant to be read anyway, windows windows windows, except the windows windows windows look out onto other windows windows windows, a grand view of the identikit building a couple of metres away, up here far removed from ground this is your choice to exist in view of others, crammed in, no light, just the life of whoever is across the way.

This is it, he says, what are we doing here. I lunge for him. Wait, he says.

And so I just stand there, he is looking for something, where the fuck is it, he says, looking and looking, there's no mess anywhere, he can't find it, whatever it is. Found it, he says, a remote control, three buttons, he presses a button, nothing happens, there is a click, nothing is happening, firmer swooshing, this is a home of swooshing, aggressive attempts at silent action, blinds blinds blinds are closing down across the windows windows windows, who would be seeing in now, who would be his audience, who is he an audience to, does he even know, does he know any of his neighbours up here in the sky, this silent shared life, unlikely, the blinds are so slow, another click finally they are down, comes to me now mouth on me hand on my arse, I can't stand he holds me arm round him I don't fall because of him. Try to make again what we had before what forty minutes ago? Can we make again what we were. Try not to think. Just relent. Pushes at me where is he pushing me going to fall, look around the couch OK we're going there I sit down I pull him down he yanks me up

   Don't mess the couch, he says.

   Pulls me I stumble he stumbles, to a door, he opens the door, swoosh and swoosh and click, scale all wrong bed too big barely any space round the edge, flatscreen on wall end of bed too big, slit of a window, light discounted, who needed light, fifty cushions at the head of the bed, looks like fifty anyway, fifty, a hundred, all plumped, he throws me down, I am part of the violence, relent, relent, relent. His shirt open his shirt off T-shirt over my head trousers down his smell everywhere his cock in my hand down my throat there is no stopping he's on me going for my arse he's going for my arse did I take my pill this morning yes I did, I did.

You have to get up.

   What. Eyes aren't opening.

   It's not a fucking hotel.

   Eyes try and be eyes. He's there, dressing. I can see from knee to waist, neatness, enforced neatness, neat trousers that sit on him neatly, a shop would call their colour olive. Neat shirt tucked into neat trousers. Vertical stripes on shirt. Trousers held up by a belt. He's putting on a sweater. Chemicals again I want to vomit oh it's cologne. He is spraying on himself chemicals to not smell like himself. Pull the cover over my ears I do not want to move cover so warm what would they call this colour in a shop, slate?

I'm serious, he says.

You don't say.

Five minutes.

What we created what we made all gone. What am I doing here don't want to be here. Fuck he pounded me good though. Can still feel it. Stay in that place. We can still be in that place. Can we.

Push back the cover I am a sewer. At least there is no light from that slit, no light can come through.

OK I'm standing up. He's there. I'm hard. He's looking at me. I stroke my cock. We can still be in that place. He's looking at me like I'm inert. He looks at me like he wants me dead.

You want to shower yourself.

I'll get one at home.

He's putting on a blazer it is so neat. That flesh now so constrained. Wait what has happened to his face. His face is neater. What has he done. Moisturized maybe. Facepack. Wait. His stubble. There's now a line. Below the line he's shaved to skin. Above the line is stubble. It's like he's trying to pretend he's not flesh. Sculpting the face. He is so boring. Crotch flattened in those trousers. Trousers chosen to neaten and to flatten his crotch. I should be dressing stand naked stare at him stand naked. No longer hard don't care stare.

Seriously he says, he's looking at me he's looking at me he's not looking at me. Reach for my jeans reach for my T-shirt, reach for my shirt they are gross as gross as me I wear what I am what does he want to hide. I am dressed I am gross. Out of the room the blinds are up he is appearing for his audience what do they see how often do they see this what is his power, his status, I do not matter I am irrelevant I do not want any role.

Work brain dammit, he says, he is fussing, he is looking for something, he cannot find something, even though there is no mess, no place for anything to be missing. Got it, he says, he pulls out of his pocket a lanyard, OK he says ready.

Sure, I say. How is a human supposed to function.

He's leaning against a counter, back to the counter, butt on the counter, he has his phone in his hand he's looking at me, what's your number he says.

Why does he want my number he hates me. I tell him my number, he types in my number, he pauses, he is not looking at me, he is looking at his phone, sorry what's your name again?

Emptiness.

How dare he.

The humiliation.

I tell him my name.

I'll message you, he says.

Wait I don't know his name.

He's left the conversation already.

I say, sure.

I do not ask his name. I want to keep us in that place. He goes to the door, he starts to open the door, I am close he comes close, mouth shut sterilized mine not, he kisses me on the lips, let's do it again, he says.

I say nothing and he doesn't care I've said nothing the door is open he is out and gone I follow I'm groggy I'm still gone how has he the pace how has he energy maybe he knows he has to fake it all day maybe he is already faking it maybe he always fakes it, maybe it's just how he is, maybe I am the one who is fake.

Down and then out and then out onto the street, road gridlocked, pavement gridlocked, he lives in gridlock, where is the river.

Which way are you going he says, I say that way. He says OK cool I'm going that way.

Anywhere other than the way I'm going.

Bye he says. Bye I say. Do we kiss what happens it is for him to decide it is his territory I don't care. He comes close and kisses quick mouth closed then looks around has anyone seen does anyone care of course they do not. Bye he says and he turns and he goes.

Watch him, watch him go, there he goes, he is becoming the others quickly he is melding that is his desire. I can see him I can see him I can't see him. Bridge in gridlock. There is the river. Over the river that place of torture celebrated for its torture. All of you stay in your place.

Wait. Jerry had lived here. Just here. One of his squats. One of his warehouses. Where we learned to be ourselves, he'd told me. He'd brought me here. When the land was rubble, when his warehouse had been demolished. Before it had become this. He had lived there and now this was what this was. What is progress.

3

More light. Two weeks since solstice. There's more light already of course there's more light it's still a surprise.

I love winter. Winter hurts me. Worked over the holidays. Prefer it. If I work Irene can be with her family. It means something to them. Let them be with their meaning. The day of that religious holiday I walked, I gardened. With Jerry we would toast the solstice and then we would just be quiet with each other over those days, while we could.

Jerry would apologize all the time, he would say he was sorry, he would say I should not have to be dealing with this. I would say that he should not have to be dealing with this, so we cancelled each other out. I would tell him I would not be anywhere else. I would tell him he had saved me.

With Jerry I learned to say what was clear and simple and elemental and true. There was no time for bullshit. There is no time for bullshit. Jerry taught me that.

We talked often about care we talked in words that were simple and clear. Jerry was angry and sad and we talked about care. We talked about care from the beginning.

That morning after the party it was just three left. Just me just Jerry just Gareth. But then Gareth was gone and so he left, I was still gone but I was awake and Jerry was caring for me.

You take anything, I remember saying it, I remember asking Jerry.

Don't want to mess with my meds, said Jerry. Not like they're doing anything for me.

We were on the couch. I had my head in Jerry's lap, I was stretched out he was sitting he was nursing me.

I knew what he was saying what he was going to say, I hoped he wouldn't say it, he said it.

I should let you know that I am HIV positive, said Jerry. He was stroking my hair, his other hand on my shoulder, he wanted me to stay where I was, no histrionics.

I said, how are you.

Right now I am well. Thank you for asking. It is kind of you to ask. I have had bad times but right now I am well. I am very well.

I looked up and Jerry looked down and he smiled and I tried to smile. It was a while before either of us said anything and then I said something.

You're the first person I've met with HIV, I said to Jerry.

Knowingly, said Jerry.

Knowingly, I said.

Jerry stroked my hair. It was soothing. Jerry soothed me.

How do you feel, said Jerry.

I told Jerry I felt sad. I told Jerry I was scared.

That is how I feel, said Jerry.

We stayed like that for a while, Jerry stroking my hair. Bodies need to move they cannot stay the same always they need to move. Jerry moved first, come on, he said. Would you like some coffee, I will make you some coffee.

I remember how useless I was. I remember his care.

I'll put on a record, he said. There were records all over the floor, their sleeves, we had been dancing, or I had been dancing, Gareth had been dancing, Jerry had been on the couch, or in the kitchen making us drinks, sometimes going out into his garden, fresh mint, he would say. It was my first time seeing the garden in daylight, not like I noticed, I was dancing. Gareth had woken by then, Gareth sat talking with Jerry and only I was dancing, and I still danced and I still danced and then I sat too. We still put on records we still put on records then Gareth said he was going, Gareth left, it was just Jerry it was just me, we still put on records, then we did not put on records then Jerry told me. And then he put on a record.

It was Grace. 'La Vie en Rose'. I love this record, I said to Jerry.

I love this record, said Jerry, he was making the coffee.

Grace sang and Grace made mood, nurtured feeling, encouraged love. I remember it so clearly. It was like that record pushed back walls, with that record we made our space and that space was beyond boundary. It was beyond boundary and it was contained by these walls, this garden. It needed definition to be beyond boundary. I remember this happening.

I was a kid, I didn't know what was happening and I remember this happening. We set our own parameters we do so by actions we do so by intentions we do so with care we do so with love. Grace sang the record played it is long. Grace took time space to set out her parameters to set out her intentions, her care, her love. This is what a record can do I have Jerry's records still I will play it now. It's Jerry's record, it creates that space. It creates that space every time. It affirms it. I get lost in it now I was lost in it then. Jerry came to the sofa with coffee, I sat up, my feet up, curled up, I sat in the middle of the sofa, I remember, I sat in the middle so Jerry would have to sit right by me, I wanted him right by me, he sat right by me he put my coffee on the floor in front of me, I put my arm around his shoulder, you stink, he said, I know, I said.

    And then we kissed.

We went upstairs after a while. Jerry holding me, me holding Jerry. Stripped off, got into Jerry's bed, it became our bed.

    We kissed. We held each other. We slept until it was dark. I woke before Jerry, his arm over me, he was pressing up into me, it was all I wanted. He was hard. He was pressing into my stomach. It was all I wanted.
My hand was on his butt, the boney thing, I brought my hand round to his cock, I held his cock, I moved
my hand on his cock, I started to jerk him off. We were face to face I was looking into his face what could I see in the dark I could see everything. I jerked him slowly like I was lulling him like he could still stay asleep. But bodies cannot stay the same they have to move I moved, I moved to get more reach, to get more hold, I moved Jerry moved, he stirred, he opened his eyes, his eyes stared, I stared, beyond staring.

    You don't have to, said Jerry.

    I want to, I said.

    Jerry closed his eyes, I kissed Jerry, we melded. Jerry flipped on his back, Jerry kicked off the cover Jerry reached for my cock I pushed his hand away I wasn't hard this wasn't about me this was about Jerry.

    He was tensing, back arching, frustration and hold on his face, he was trying to stop something and start something, keep something going and let it be over, eyes clenched, maybe he was thinking about me, most likely not, it's OK, most likely he was thinking of someone else, some other guy, or guys, some other scenario, real or imagined, both, a fiction of something real, it didn't matter, he wouldn't be able to say, he wouldn't know how to explain, that's not what words are. He came on his stomach, hard and strong. He came and as he came Jerry halted his breath and caught his breath and laughed and then Jerry cried. My head next to his head I kissed the side of his head I smoothed his hair we lay there we lay there till the cum dried we laid there beyond.

It was dark I had no idea what time it was where was my watch. I was in our bed alone. It was our bed already. I could hear Jerry downstairs. I was cold I was warm the ecstasy was leaving my bloodstream I knew what was happening. Still I was warm I was cold I wanted rest I was restless.

    I tried to stand, stood. Jerry must have heard me. He shouted up.

    I left out some sweatpants for you, a sweater, he said. Your clothes stink.

    It would become what we said. You stink. Your clothes stink. Your breath stinks. Your arsehole stinks. We stink.

    Went downstairs, in Jerry's clothes. Jerry was in the kitchen, Jerry was cooking. Hey, said Jerry.

    Hey, I said.

Hope you're hungry.

I'm hungry.

I didn't know what to do, I knew what to do, I was a kid.

Do you want to put on a record?

Sure, I said. I went to his records, I flicked through his records, there were records I knew there were records I did not know there were records I wanted to know. Pulled out a record I had on cassette, it was by Joni, I put on the record by Joni, *Court and Spark*.

Perfect, said Jerry.

I had this cassette I had listened to this cassette it had chewed up it had gnarled I still played the cassette but now I didn't need the cassette we had the record.

What time is it.

Gone nine, said Jerry. Would you like some wine? I am going to have a glass of wine.

Please, I said. So set our domesticity. Jerry cooked me pasta, to soak it all up, he said. It was simple, pasta, tomatoes, garlic. I grew the tomatoes, said Jerry, it's my sauce.

Jerry's sauce was delicious.

The red wine fugged me nicely. I was curled on the sofa again, I was a kid, Jerry was a kid. We'd get up to turn the record, change the record, to get more wine, soon I was nodding, eyes closing when I didn't want my eyes to close, I could not help it, my eyes wanted to close.

You can stay here if you want, said Jerry, his hand was on my arm, our feet, our legs locked together.

That would be so nice, I said.

I had to be in college by nine. Jerry said he started work at nine thirty. We went to bed, we held each other, we kissed, we slept, I slept and I slept and I slept. It was simple. In the morning I showered and Jerry made me coffee, made a bowl of yoghurt, oats, honey, cinnamon. He slid open the garden door. He stood outside. I joined him. It was cold.

Thank you, Jerry said.

Thank you, I said.

Went back up to my flat, put on some clothes, got my books, my pen, my paper. It was a couple of months before I officially moved into Jerry's, before I stopped paying rent on the flat I hated, the flat with the ex-friend, my friend from before I understood friendship.

But really that morning I had all but moved out. I spent every night at Jerry's, every day, after a couple of weeks he gave me a key. Well you pretty much live here now, he said. Do you want to move your stuff?

And so I did.

4

Sounds a keeper, dear.

Gareth is sat in his chair and Gareth is as exact as ever, Gareth still close shaven Gareth's hair clipped and creamed, Gareth's sweater is specific. It is navy. Gareth's jeans are indigo and have suffered no wear. The turn-up is specific and it is fixed. A cane is on the floor, exactly in line with the chair. Maude is on Gareth's lap, Maude is always on Gareth's lap. Round Gareth's chair are piles of books, each one exact, the piles of books radiate out from him, each pile put together with specific meaning that only concerns Gareth. I am in the chair I always sit in, the chair nearby his with its own piles radiating outwards. You're non-fiction dear, Gareth said to me once, around me books on antiquities and on tapestry and on Paganism and on the occult. I'm pure fiction, said Gareth, his piles Baldwin and Austen and Isherwood and Forster and Butler and Le Guin and Dostoevsky and Orwell and and and. Floor painted grey no dust visible. A rug. Warm outside. Gareth always has the heating so hot in here. Three of Jerry's paintings on the wall, I like him here with me, Gareth says, Gareth always says it, whenever I visit. I always say to Gareth, me too. I've just said it.

Check in on Gareth every week. His flat is close to the

surgery. Get him shopping run errands pick up his prescription. Gareth's flat is on the first floor there's no lift it's becoming more of a problem Gareth is putting off the problem by staying as exact as he can. He says, when I let myself go they can take me away.

I love Gareth I love gossiping with Gareth I love remembering with Gareth. Gareth keeps me close to Jerry. Gareth keeps himself close to Jerry, Gareth now sounds like Jerry, like he's being Jerry, or maybe that's just age, maybe that's just how words go, Jerry so old to me then, Gareth now old.

I have a tea Gareth has a tea. A pot on the table between us. Milk jug. Been telling him about that guy whose name I cannot remember.

And you still don't know his name, Gareth says.

I still don't know his name.

Whatever happened to civility, Gareth says, he is smiling teeth bared, he's spent a life of nights on the heath, he knows anonymity, he knows civility.

He messaged, I say. I am getting out my phone, open the message, read it exactly, 'that was fun mate let's do it again x'. He didn't say his name.

You're not going to do it again, says Gareth. My face is talking I don't need words. Gareth is reading me, Gareth is smiling, Gareth says, you're going to do it again.

He was awful, I say, Why is everybody now so awful.

My dear boy everybody was always awful, Gareth says. It's just that nowadays everybody has more opportunity to reveal their awfulness.

Maude has not moved Maude does not move.

Everybody was always awful. In my day awful queens just hid behind so-ci-et-y.

Gareth likes to stretch out a word that he can stretch out.

So-ci-et-y was really just a construction to let awful queens get away with whatever they wanted and be awful. Have I ever told you about that cottage near Parliament.

Gareth has often told me about that cottage near Parliament I love it when he tells me about the cottage near Parliament.

An MP would be sucking me off one minute and then next minute he would be back in the chamber casting his millionth vote against the vile sin of homo-sex-ual-it-y. His mouth full of my spunk and then he's running off to jolly well make sure we all remained repressed. Or a lord. A lord with a mouthful of my cum. Because that is all they knew, repression, it suited them, they had the power they craved. They could only maintain their grip on power by keeping their desires hidden. But they couldn't give a damn about free expression of anything. Anyway their public-school breeding meant they were only turned on by the illicit. And so you see everybody has always been awful. Today's awful people just need to find new ways to be awful ever since our desires became . . .

He pauses.

Normal.

He is laughing and he is stroking Maude and Maude does not move.

I spent my life doing everything I could to fight normality and where do we find ourselves. Normality. What a vic-tor-y. Dear, did you get any biscuits, I would love a biscuit.

There are biscuits, I got us biscuits.

Because of course normal men are all awful. To become one of them, to become normal, us queers need to be awful every moment of every day.

I say, not everyone is awful.

Everyone who wasn't awful died, dear. With them went a way of being. Community, fairness, sharing, decency. We had very serious intentions which we wore with light-ness.

Gareth lingered over the word light-ness, it was almost light. ness.

That light-ness was very important to us, and it made it easy for everyone to not take us seriously. Our light-ness showed our se-rious-ness. Then people started dying and we had to fight and we had to get angry and the light-ness was all gone. Jerry was one of the last dear, wasn't he.

Jerry was the first man I loved, I say, and the first man I loved who died.

You were such a fragile little thing, Gareth says, and so sharp.

Ha, I say to Gareth, yeah right I was sharp, I was just some idiot kid.

You knew what you were doing.

I had no clue what I was doing only that I did not want to do what I had been doing and that I wanted to do whatever Jerry was doing. OK I knew what I was doing I just never admit to myself I know what I'm doing.

You found each other and you saved him.

He saved me.

It was mutual and it was beautiful. Jerry had given up hope before he met you. You gave him life those last few years. He didn't even make 50. It is so cruel. You now carry him within you.

I don't, I don't do him justice I fail him I fail him every day I've failed him Gareth.

Gareth looks at me and looks at me.

How do you think Jerry would be living if he were alive today, if he had been able to live, if his life had been what it should always have been? He would still be doing exactly the same as you until his sorry old carcass could take no more. He would be living life just like you. What would Jerry be doing if he were the hot new young thing in town right now? He would be running wild and free. What would Jerry hate if he were alive today? For you to be turning him into some saint, for you to be holding him up as this messianic figure, for you to be doubting yourself, for you to be comparing yourself to him. You know Jerry, you know him really, Jerry was unlike anyone I have ever met. Jerry was the best human and Jerry was a mess and Jerry had enemies and Jerry was fallible and he did not run from it he revelled in it. It is a nightmare that he died so young we are living in a nightmare, but it is even more of a nightmare if you forget who he really was. If we turn those who have died into saints, what does it do? It makes everything cosy, it ties everything up, because they may have died but wait it's all OK they're saints now, they're above us all, they have transcended, they have escaped their nightmare, and so then the real nightmare disappears, we forget the nightmare, and we cannot forget the nightmare, Johnny, we cannot forget it. If you turn him into a saint, you acquiesce. Do you understand what I'm saying, Johnny, I am old, my brain is old, I cannot always keep my train of thought. It is so clear to me, and yet I find it so hard to explain.

I think I understand, I say to him.

Do you remember that time?, says Gareth. Maybe it didn't strike you because you were so young, you weren't to know. We were all exhausted, all of us who survived, everyone was exhausted. Everyone wanted the nightmare to be over. Everyone wanted to live normal lives. Everyone wanted to forget about everything. It is understandable, you cannot blame anyone for it. But here is the thing, Johnny. Before the nightmare began, the last thing we wanted was normality. Our lives were dedicated to the pursuit of queer magic.

He stretched out the words. Qu-ee-er mmm-ag-ic.

It was queer magic that reached back through time, reached far into the future, it broke time, it broke the physical realm, it broke the constraints of what is considered normal, that awful world of conformity where really you just become a cog in the machine, where you are milked for profit, where your primary role is to consume and therefore be consumed. AIDS put queer magic in total jeopardy. So much magic wiped out. We have to reconnect with queer magic today or else all is lost.

Gareth sips his tea. Gareth bites his biscuit. Gareth sips his tea. I say nothing, Gareth has not finished, his thoughts are still loose and free, this is intelligence, not academia, not cleverness, this is intelligence, being able to set thoughts loose and free, the bravery, the lack of fear, the nerve and the patience to set thoughts loose and free where they might falter, to let them instead head into full flight, to expand and unravel and reveal themselves and reveal their contradictions and their complexities and their paradoxes and maybe the thoughts become a new plane of realization, maybe that plane is never reached but the attempt is worth it, the attempt takes time, Gareth takes time and so goes beyond time. Gareth sips his tea.

This is how you honour Jerry, says Gareth and he is speaking into new air. Can you see? By connecting with queer magic. By resisting normality. By caring. By coming here, every week, to spend this time with me, by being here, you know how much it means to me, Johnny, that you come here, that you care enough to sit here and be bored rigid by this dried-up old dragon.

Gareth is staring at me as he says this and is smiling.

I am never bored rigid by you Gareth, I say and I mean it, though Gareth is sometimes boring, sometimes says the same thing over and over, often says the same thing over and over, repeats himself, goes over the same stories, treads the same ground, sometimes he is boring and that is OK I am never bored by him, I am never bored rigid.

If we normalize Jerry's death, we eradicate Jerry. We eradicate him. If we normalize the nightmare of HIV, the nightmare of our lives, we eradicate its victims, because so many of its victims lived a life that was anything but normal. It is so normal to say someone is a saint. I hate normality. Anyway dear you know what I think, you've heard me say it so many times, right now it's pretty much only you left that will listen. And Maude.

Maude has not moved.

Keep doing what you are doing, Johnny my dear boy, Jerry would be proud of you, Jerry is proud of you, keep living life as you are living life, keep making mistakes, keep fucking up, keep being glorious. Go and see that awful man again, he sounds so awful. Do make sure you come and tell me all about it, won't you. You know I like to be kept up to speed. All the news that's fit to print.

5

It is Saturday, I am making bread, it is what I do on a Saturday, I make bread I make stock. The mother has lived here longer than me, Jerry introduced me to the mother, showed me how to feed the mother, I have been feeding the mother ever since, if I go away Nasim feeds the mother, I do not have a pet I have the mother. When I eat the bread I eat the same bread Jerry made. It is the same bread, Jerry is here with me. It is as simple as that, it is as clear and as real and as alive as that. The bread I make is never that good, it is always a bit too heavy, it is not fancy bread. It is the bread that I make and it is the same as the bread that Jerry made. Nasim always panics, what if I kill the mother? It's OK, we'd start a new mother. It's OK.

The guy whose name I can't remember hasn't messaged back he said he'd message back. He said he wanted to see me today he said, I want your hole, I said, OK, that was two days ago, today is the day he said he'd want my hole, he's not messaged back. I've got no other plans it's OK.

The stock I make with whatever scraps have been left over from the week, onion skins, celery ends, stalks of parsley, whatever. Jerry taught me how to make stock, it is the same stock I make every week that Jerry made every week, each week it is a new stock, it is the same stock that Jerry made, it's OK.

The stock is on the back light the light that keeps the temperature steady it's the same cooker it still works. I'm kneading the dough I'm kneading the dough I'm kneading the dough.

It was a Saturday, we were making pizza, I was trying to knead dough.

The heel of your hand, Jerry said, no the heel, the heel, let me show you.

This was a lesson, learn the lesson, I didn't know then I was meant to learn the lesson. I was in a field of happiness, I was terrified, I hid my terror, Jerry knew I was terrified, Jerry knew I was hiding it, he was the same. It was unbearable, that these could exist together, happiness and the terror. Before I had been a child, I was now facing this conflict, what it was to be adult, I had to bear it.

I'd been moved in a few weeks. We had settled quick into time out of time. Before I met Jerry time had been ordered, allotted, wasted, the waste of teenage years, no friends, isolation, my first year in the city a waste, presuming the city would solve everything, not realizing that to be in the city you had to make it work, you had to be a participant, the banality of that year before I met Jerry, wasted in student dorms, basic bars, friends of convenience and chance and desperation, college was a joke, who cared what they taught me, I didn't care, it was all a waste of time, that time wasted was a weight, it weighed on me, time wasted a physical burden, I couldn't bear it.

The anxiety of time wasted. It is what I had lived with and then I met Jerry and then it disappeared. This is what Jerry gave me. We existed outside time. We had our commitments, Jerry his mornings working at the community centre, which often became his afternoons, afternoons getting in people's shopping, doing repairs for people, or just visiting, just sitting, just talking. He helped a family fight deportation. They were not deported. Their son still lives on the estate. Racists threw dogshit at his neighbour's door. Jerry cleaned the dogshit. The racists threw dogshit whenever they found dogshit, everyone knew who they were, they lived upstairs, no one stopped them, Jerry always cleaned it for his neighbour, whenever he saw the dogshit the racists had thrown. Jerry tried to get the police to care, they could not care. Jerry tried to get the council to care, they could not care. Jerry working into his own time, whatever needed doing, Jerry did it.

    I had college worked out, I knew which classes took register, which I could miss, I missed as much as I could and still I missed nothing, all I needed to learn was here, Flat 1, Nova Scotia House, what more did I need. And so it was a Saturday evening, already into our rhythm, it could have been any evening, every evening as valued as the other, as normal as the other in its value, no grandeur, no grandstanding, just care.

    We had spent the day sweeping up leaves, tidying edges. If the edges are tidy you don't need to care about the rest, said Jerry. Darkness was falling hard, winter now determined, no longer a threat, Jerry ran a bath, he had it scalding, I could not get into what he got into. He got in, he suffered that heat, he said he enjoyed it. I played him a record, the bathroom door open so he could hear it fully, Alice Coltrane, both sides of *Journey in Satchidananda*, after a while we swapped, I got in the water when he'd finished, still boiling to me, it's freezing, he said. He brought me some wine, lit a candle, put it by the bath, came and sat with me, that was good work today, he said. My dick was hard, it always was in the bath, at that age, mind if I, I said, he laughed and he said be my guest, and so I started to jerk myself off, it turned me on that Jerry was watching, I turned him on, I took my time, felt down to my arsehole, put a finger in, two, nice, Jerry said. And then I had to do it, arched my back out of the water, I came hard, cum hit my face, fuck, said Jerry, he came too, came on his belly, kept it on his belly, that hairy belly, cum catcher, that's how it was.

The record finished. Jerry stood, wiped off the cum with the T-shirt he'd been wearing, put on trackpants, a sweater, socks. He kissed me, smiled, headed downstairs, put on a record, I didn't know it, I shouted, what's this? Billy, he said, Billy Strayhorn.

'Love Came'. I put my head under the water to cope. I'd stay submerged if I could. I had to surface. Congealed cum stuck in my hairs. The water cooled, I finished my wine, I could hear Jerry pottering, my favourite new sound, what a lie the talk of love eternal, this sound was finite, Jerry would die, we did not have long.

I could smell onions. Got out, dried myself, went downstairs, kissed Jerry. Let's get started, he said.

Jerry showed me how to make the dough. OK now mix it, he said. I went to the drawer to get a wooden spoon.

No. Use your hands.

Brought the dough together, OK knead it, he said, and he showed me how. I asked him how long for. He said, You'll know.

There was no recipe book open. How did he know what to do.

You remember the most useless stuff, he said. Who did he mean by you. You meaning himself, you meaning me, who knew, both true.

Where do you know it from, I said. I just know it, he said, which was flippant and he knew it and I knew it, and I waited for the real story to come, I was learning, just wait and the real story always comes.

That's enough, he said. Jerry oiled a baking tray, OK now press the dough into it. The dough was springy, tense, it wouldn't relent, it relented. First went on anchovies, then cheese. Now the sauce, he said. He had a tomato sauce simmering with the onions. He said, all from the garden. Jerry said he made gallons of tomato sauce every September. Sees him through the winter. We'll make it together, he said, next September.

He looked at me as he said it, it was the look of the determined, I will still be alive next September, won't I, you will still be with me next September, won't you, you won't leave me, what we have is real, I want you to stay, do not leave me, that was all in the look. Will I be alive will I be here, I want to be alive, I want to be here.

I said to Jerry, I cannot wait to make it with you in September, and I kissed him and I held him, what did I know, what did I know.

The real story came, I just had to wait, Jerry started telling me his story, parts of his story he'd already told me, in other ways, as parts of other stories, we were always telling each other stories, this is the story he told me that Saturday night, he was spreading the tomato sauce on top of the cheese, isn't it the wrong way round, I said, no, he said, it's the right way. This is the way I was taught, he said, when I was young. This is what I know.

He took a sip of wine and he started. Of course I got out of this country as soon as I could, he said. I escaped. No one cared that I'd gone. They were glad to see the back of me. I travelled. I learned to do this on my travels.

He was sprinkling breadcrumbs on top, a batch he had stored, toasted, then some dried oregano, shaken, from a bunch.

Now we leave it to rise, he said. It'll be a couple of hours. The good things take time.

We got on the sofa, sat either end, legs entwined, how did I find you, said Jerry. How did I find you, I said.

By your age I'd escaped, said Jerry. I went to Europe and I travelled in Europe and I lived in Europe. I had no money but then I did not need money. I hitched. I stayed on people's floors. If I needed money I washed dishes. And that way I learned how people lived and how people survived, what they lived through, what they would accept, how you could be. I knew I did not want to live in any way like my parents, or my parents' parents, my friends, their parents, anyone I knew. There was nobody I knew who I wanted to be like. I wanted to break from everything, their cycles, their practices, their religion, their assumptions, their rules, their order. I was done with it all. And so I escaped.

When was this, I said, I had his foot in my hand, I was massaging it, the dark ages, he said. The nineteen sixties. When I was travelling, I found a way of being, but you must understand me, there was no big revelation, there was no big theory, no alternative, it was just living in a very simple way, a very humble way, and also in a very primal way, it was very much connected to sex, and the men I was sleeping with, the men I was being fucked by, it was very normal to them, to sleep with men, it was no drama, they didn't seem troubled by their desire, it was so liberating, and it was elemental. And for me it connected with everything else that was elemental, with food, with friendship, with labour, with seasonality, with nature. It was my education, I educated myself in a way of living that was natural to me. It is how I have always tried to live since.

Where did you travel.

Anywhere by the sea. I liked the sea. I liked what the sea did to men. It liberated them. Maybe I wouldn't have slept with so many if it hadn't been for the sea. Maybe I just had the gift of the gab.

Married men?

Married men, priests, sailors, soldiers, artists, poets, cooks, musicians, whoever, I kept diaries, they are all listed, I wrote it all down, the diaries brought me more men, I'd be writing my diary in a bar, I was such a trim young innocent little thing, writing in all innocence, I'd make eye contact with some guy or other, didn't matter who, it was all I had to do. I'd carry on writing, and in a moment they would be over, asking questions, and it was clear what they wanted, what I would be for them, a release, I loved it.

Jerry had brought a bottle of wine to the sofa, he poured me more, poured himself some too.

At that time, many of us were questioning ways of living. There was a softness about life, a possibility, a generosity, if you found it for yourself, but for many this questioning was a fad, or a lie, when I came back to this country I was always called a hippy and I didn't know what to make of it. I was just trying to live life in my own way, it was of no concern to anyone else, but it was like I scared them. It's why I had left this country in the first place. I wanted to get away from a society that imposes itself upon you, it is what I have struggled with since, some might say I've failed.

All I could do was smile at him, a smile lips closed, closed to try and show sympathy, what could I say, what can you say to someone who thinks they have failed, only they know the standard by which they judge themselves, the impossible standard that they can never meet, self-imposed so that they never meet it, so they always consider themselves to have failed, what can you say, all I could say was, I know what you mean.

Jerry smiled at me and said, it's hard not to.

Why didn't you stay abroad.

I heard from friends, they had started squatting in warehouses back here, down by the river, it seemed like a place we could do something interesting. And I wanted to see if I could bring the way of living I had found to the country where I was born. And so I came back. And we lived in those warehouses until they were torn down. I shared my life with artists, with writers, with dancers, with filmmakers, and I brought all I had learned back with me and I grew all I could on the roof, and I fed us for next to nothing, and that food, that crop, those harvests, that connection to a way of living was at the heart of our queerness. And this is the important thing. It wasn't queerness in opposition to straight people. It wasn't about trying to find a place within straight society at all. It was queerness for and of itself, and it was fertile, creative, it was bounteous. Really it was glorious. I used to be embarrassed talking about it but now I can face what we did clearly and talk of it with clarity. I am sure I am now meant to mock what we did, to belittle it, to be embarrassed by it, or say we were only young, that we were idealistic, that we were naïve, that we were hiding rather than engaging with the world, that we were bums, I'm sure I'm meant to say all these things, others who I lived with said these things when they had entered straight society, they trivialized what we did, and because it gets trivialized, now really no one knows what we did. But we did something. It was queerness, for and of itself. It was glorious. It has gone. And now pretty much everyone is dead. But the way of living can happen again. I know it can happen again.

Jerry took a sip of wine and he breathed.

It was very simple and very humble and very serious and very fun. That was my twenties and my thirties. All you have. Ahead of you.

He said it like a dare. He said it with a sadness, his acceptance that I could not meet that dare, because what can grow when the roots have been pulled out. He said it like it was his fault, that he had failed.

I said to him, what I have ahead with you.

My voice was timid but I meant it. This was what we did, we sat and we talked and we cooked. It was so simple, there was nothing special, that is what made it special, it was so other, we were mapping our world while we could, while Jerry still could.

There was a pause, long. Are you OK, said Jerry, he was always checking if I was OK, it should have been the other way round, but he was always checking, always making sure, he cared, I'm really OK, I said to him. I'd moved in just a few weeks before, a few weeks, so much time, who needs time.

Are you sure, you can tell me, I must be so boring, you could be having so much fun.

He said this even though I had told him and told him and told him how bored I'd been before we'd met, I told him again, I had come to the city expecting everything and finding nothing, how with him I had finally found something, he said, yes you've found the one last sorry carcass standing.

He smiled again like a dare. I tried to meet his dare but I could not meet his dare. I stood and I went to the record player and tried to find a record I wanted to play but could not find a record to play. I could not look at him.

Johnny, you have to let me laugh, he said, you have to let me have my humour, without it I would be lost, what am I, a bag of old bones, I should be put out with the trash, I don't know why you bother.

6

Spring. I live my life like I am on a cliff and any moment I could fall off the cliff.

Liz emailed, checking in, just making sure the council haven't been round I can't believe we get away with it after all these years. When Jerry died the council wanted me out they wouldn't let it pass to someone who wasn't blood they didn't recognize unmarried partners we could not be married it was illegal we did not exist. Jerry's sister Liz said she lives here says she lives here. I sublet. But I do not know of any other way of living this is all I know. I do my work I am good at my work I don't know any other work I believe my work is important work I want to keep doing my work. Who can I turn to, the council? Government? Charity? I do not know what to do I will do what I always do I will let it all come crashing over me.

All I have is here in this flat this is all I know. But I never want to cling, it is not about sentimentality, it is about being, it is about trying to be. Being is hard being gets harder unless you live in ways I don't agree with. I don't agree with those ways I can't do it this is the way I can live. What else can I do.

Who else lives this way is there anyone left can they help

me are they all gone. I live with the work of those who once lived this way. Still got the couch. No nostalgia. Jerry hated nostalgia. I hate nostalgia. It's a good couch. Friends of Jerry's made it. Ugly to some eyes. Wild. Railway sleepers. Deep low seat. Rope from by the water. Rope held together the back and sides. Headpiece rising at the back, carved with the sun, the sun wild, squirming.

  His friends made the chair, simple, wide, ugly to some, ugly because it was one-off, off-kilter, ugly because it was never new, made from old, it was always off, off in its scale, too big then too small, looked like it might tumble, slightly too low slightly too deep. You think it'll be uncomfortable until you sit in it and then it is everything.

  His friends made our bed too, simple, no drama, low, broad, more like a platform, a solid stable dependable platform for love for trust for honesty, honest of design, the intention of the design, the intentions of the designers, Jerry's friends, becomes the intentions of its use, it cost nothing, all the wood found, a headboard that was low and carved in the centre with a hard cock and a heart, the cock and the heart wild, squirming.

I'll show you where they had their studio, Jerry said one day, haven't been that way in ages. I'd been moved in a while, a good few months, it was on my mind, Jerry had not said he loved me, I had not said I love you, it made me anxious, wasn't that what you were supposed to do, what were you supposed to do, I did not know what you were supposed to do. Maybe I was seeking comfort in normality, like it could help, like anything could help. It went round and round in my mind, what did I know I knew nothing.

I'd been asking Jerry about the sofa, the chair, the bed, friends made them, he'd say, it was all he'd say, he didn't want to say, it hurt too much, I was yet to experience this hurt, its depths, its breadth, how Jerry was expected to just deal with it, expected by who, no one caring, family not caring, establishment not caring, government not caring, the Church not caring, newspapers not caring, no one cared and Jerry, everyone sick, everyone affected, was expected to just deal with it. I was soon expected just to deal with it.

He'd got on his waterproof, thick sweater beneath. Let's go, he said.

We headed north.

Be careful, he said.

We had crossed the road, were approaching a pub, painted white, the flag of the country in its window, the flag of the country painted on the grill in the pavement outside, two men stood by its door,

Don't look, said Jerry.

We turned left, went down its side, when we had passed it Jerry said, pub for racists, and then he said, we live in a society where there can be a pub for racists. And they can display their racism to all and to everyone. They are allowed to be. And we are left to rot.

We were silent for a while. I was scared. Jerry walked with his usual purpose. I had not walked this way before, up, away. Estates in worse states than ours. Blocks derelict. Blocks of rubble.

Still not cleared from the war, said Jerry, this land is worth less than nothing.

Luxury flats on that land now, I know the block, I know the flats, got fucked by a guy in one when they were new, they're not so new now, bet an apartment goes for what around seven hundred and fifty thousand. Rubble then, rubble, grass growing through the rubble. A street market with no market, the street still called a market even though there was no market, no money in it, no money in the neighbourhood to shop at it, suddenly a quaint old church, quaint like it was in a village where barely anyone lived and barely anything happened, this quaint village church suddenly found itself here in this desolation, this abandon, four quaint houses next to it, not bombed, the three quaint houses keeping their friend the quaint church safe, coddled, it's OK quaint church, it's OK, the damage that the Church has done, the violence, the suppression, it's OK quaint church, it's OK.

Onto a main road, someone walked past us and when they had gone past us Jerry said, how charming, and I said, what, and he said, they never even acknowledge me any more. He didn't say anything else about the person, I knew not to ask, it often happened, we'd see someone and Jerry would say, look away, or, let's steer clear of him, or, that ship has long set sail. The door is closed, he would say of former friends or, they are off the radar. Jerry was gregarious and Jerry loved people and he was also terrible with people, he cut them off, couldn't allow for their fallibility, expected too much from them, or maybe he was just frightened of friendship, he had friends he had many friends but then there were many who fell away or who cut him off too, he had no remorse he was done they were gone that was it.

The person was behind us, it was us two together alone among millions. We headed due north, the road scary and strict, shops empty, shops derelict, on the street in front blankets laid on the ground, people selling whatever they could to whoever wanted it, old books, old clothes, old toys, someone trying to sell old radios, old televisions, someone else old dolls, hair matted and wild, someone else snowglobes, hundreds of them, all lined up in rows, on a blanket, on the floor, Jerry stopped to look, said to the man selling the snowglobes, why snowglobes?

Mum died, said the man selling the snowglobes.

We kept walking.

Almost there, said Jerry.

Other side of the road, left, down a sharp diagonal, going down, a sharp diagonal among the straights.

It was here, said Jerry, you wouldn't know it now.

Two shops boarded up. Windows upstairs boarded up, no life, no signs there was ever life, it's still like that now, went by the other week.

Those boys, those poor boys, said Jerry. Seems so long ago.

When was it, I said.

Six years ago, seven, he said.

Jerry had been Jerry on the walk but it was like Jerry was retreating into himself. He coughed, said he was cold, said he was tired. Uncomfortable with himself, with what had happened, he had not told me what had happened. I got Jerry to a greasy spoon, seats stuck to the table, table stuck to the floor, plastic. Very modern, said Jerry.

I got Jerry tea and he started to tell me about them. It was so glorious, Jerry said, it was so sad.

I had a bacon sandwich. Jerry said he wasn't hungry. I was hungry.

We knew each other from the squats, said Jerry. No one

cared what we did, no one paid us any attention. We were kids but we were doing something. We were setting new ways of being and those new ways of being were based on gay love, on queer respect, and on a total rejection of the straight life that had been imposed on us through our childhoods. I do not say lightly that what we were doing was new.

He paused, like he was waiting for something, something he knew was coming and couldn't do anything about it, he had fear in his eyes, and then he coughed, he coughed and he coughed, he waited, he coughed, waited, it seemed to pass, he still waited, he waited.

When he started again, his voice was softer, I do not say this lightly, he said again, I think about this often. There was no precedent. No one acknowledges this now, of course, no one cares. I sound crazy talking about it. I sound crazy whenever I talk about it. People roll their eyes. Yadda yadda. Maybe I should just sip my tea and shut up.

I stared at him and I smiled. I took a bite of my bacon sandwich. It was delicious. I was learning to live in the pauses, to resist the need to talk, Jerry left long pauses, often. It would seem like he had left a thought, an opinion, an argument halfway through, like he had trailed off. He hadn't. To begin with I would say something into the pause, embarrassed by the pause, and Jerry would look at me annoyed like I'd broken a spell. I had broken a spell. And then I realized the pause was part of what was being said. That the pause allowed Jerry to consider what to say next. That the pause allowed what had already been said to have its presence and have its effect. Jerry would always say something again, even if it was just a couple of words to show that actually, the thought had reached its end point. It was a decency he afforded me too, a respect for words, a respect for the brain, for whatever it was doing, a respect for thinking. Jerry paused. Jerry paused and Jerry sipped some more tea and then Jerry continued.

Of course it took its toll, Jerry said, trying to do something new, rejecting the norm. In the end it was the end for them. It was too much. It was too much.

Jerry sipped some more tea.

Michael started making furniture when we shared a warehouse, down by the river. To begin with we found our furniture on the street, broken, mouldy. Michael hated it. Michael said it reminded him of everything from which he had escaped. He said it reminded him of everything he didn't want to be. He said, we could do better. He said, we can make furniture that works for us. He said he could make furniture so that we could live.

Another sip of tea.

We were born in dark times dear. We grew up in mean homes, and these homes had been built for mean lives. A mean little kitchen that was solely mother's domain, her trap for life. A mean little dining room for father to lord it over the family. A mean little sitting room for us to be entertained by what was spoon-fed to us, first on the radio and then when they could afford it on television. It was a miserable way of living and I wanted nothing to do with it. Luckily they wanted nothing to do with me so that was pretty clear.

Jerry paused, no sip of tea.

When I met Michael, when I moved in with all of that community, it was clear that it wasn't just our sexuality that was different, it was the structure of our lives, it was our entire way of living. It wasn't just how we formed relationships or formed communities, it was the very fabric of our lives that could be different, the very furniture. Literally. It was a contradiction to live with new principles but still live in a miserable two up two down with its toxic assumptions of how life should be lived and who had control. The homes we had grown up in were physical manifestations of everything we rejected.

The warehouses gave us the chance to redraw. To redraw the way we lived. Maybe not everybody in the community recognized the importance of what we were doing, maybe some were just in it for the ride, for the parties, for the boys, for the drugs. I had no problem with them. They made life fun. But for Michael and me it was also something very serious. We lived in three of them. The first was a dummy run, really, it was a shambles. But then we realized what we were doing and we got serious about our shambles. We would talk and we would talk about what it meant to be gay and to live. Not hiding in plain sight, not being ashamed, not acquiescing, not apologetic, how did we want to live.

Jerry took the last sip of his tea. He looked at me and he said, shall we have another dear.

I liked being a dear. Got us two more cups, 50p each. From an urn. I sat back down and Jerry was ready to talk again straight away Jerry was ready.

Michael and I talked about everything, and by everything I obviously mean who we fucked and who we were fucking and it could be a friend or a stranger it could be the man we wished could be our lover for life it didn't matter, what mattered was our respect and our tolerance for each other, and that sounds free and easy but actually it takes hard work to be free and we were willing to work hard, to us it was exciting and it was natural and it was how life should be.

Jerry tried the tea, it was still too hot. He held the cup tight, he wanted its warmth.

But what we talked about went beyond who we were fucking we talked about everything how everything should be. One day Michael came back with some wood he'd found and said he was going to make us a discussion platform. We'd been sitting on miserable old sofas that had been dumped on the street, miserable mean things that made you think misery was comfort. He built a platform that was low and wide, this vast square, raised from the ground, it was a defined space for comfort and for engagement, covered with a rug of woven hemp which was very fitting for us as I'm sure you'll imagine.

Jerry sipped some tea.

It took a couple of attempts. All his materials were found. He had to stabilize it, I do believe it was after I had used the platform for something other than discussion. Nigel who had joined the squat made the cushions that we sat on and leaned on and reclined on, he called it a modular system, which was a fancy name for something that worked. It was wonderful. It always felt like an occasion, just being on the platform. We would look forward to being on the discussion platform. We would spend whole days on the discussion platform. We had a record player in the warehouse and so of course at night the discussion platform turned into a fabulous dancefloor. It was also a stage when necessary. David made some of his early films using the discussion platform. Then when they demolished that warehouse, we took it apart and took it with us to the next warehouse. And then we had to move out of that warehouse, and we could find no more warehouses.

Why was that, I said.

They realized that the unwanted worlds in which we had made our homes would one day be worth something. But they wouldn't be worth anything with us still in them, trying to be different. They needed us gone, and when we were gone, they torched the place. Insurance.

We splintered. It was time. I moved to a squat in town. Michael moved up here. But everything we had discussed, everything we had experienced, everything we had learned still applied, it still mattered, it would always apply, it would always matter.

Others had joined our table, sitting on their own plastic chair attached to the plastic table, then they had gone, someone else sat down, ate, left, the café busy then not busy then busy, transient.

Jerry carried on talking and these other people did not bother him.

Michael soon formed what was really a loose collective, he said. A collective because they helped each other and shared the same beliefs and sparked each other, they created their own world, it was such a thrill, the clothes, the shoes, the furniture, the brooches from bones, old bones they scavenged from down by the river, everything scavenged from somewhere, all old made new, the unloved loved, it became their own world, all with the same values and the same integrity of making something from nothing.

But they were a loose collective because really they were stoned most of the time. It was a miracle they ever got anything done. They had a shop that was never open. I mean, never open. If you banged on the door someone may have answered you, maybe. If they were open, they had nothing to sell. That was the point of what they were doing. They were committed to a way of living and a way of creating and producing that was the opposite of the cut-throat and the mercenary way of being that had taken over society. They refused to compromise their ideals. Michael started to make pieces that looked like they might fall over. He wanted whoever saw them to feel unease, because he was against pretending the world was comfortable and comforting and that really elegance was just piss and shit, that is what he would say. Elegance is just piss and shit. He realized that he could jolt the brain into action with his work, it is like a constant electric charge. They were really standing against everything else that was happening at the time. I loved them. I loved their work. So little of it survives. So few of them survived.

What happened, I said.

It was very hard for all of them. It was very beautiful what they were doing and it was very hard. And it only got harder. It was dark times. Michael was using by then and he said he had it under control but of course he didn't. Nobody did. And one day he overdosed. And he died. He was 34. It was the saddest thing. And I cannot help but feel he intended to do it. To me it did not feel like an accident. I think it was all too much for him and he made the decision. Which I think upsets some people but it is what I think. Why try and sugar coat.

Jerry stared at me to tell me all he couldn't say. What he told me by staring at me went beyond conversation and went beyond time and went beyond linear thought he was telling me something I could not tell you what he was telling me he was telling me something for me to tell you what he told me by staring at me I would have to stare at you to tell you something that I could not say that is the only way.

It is horrible to think there was no other way for him, Jerry said, but they were totally opposed to what was shiny and what was new and by then the world thought it was obsessed with what was shiny and new, which really meant corporations kept finding clever ways to make us think we are obsessed with what is shiny and new. We are not obsessed. We are conned into feeling like we are obsessed. And it was very difficult for Michael to keep going when nearly everyone around him was falling for this obsession with what was shiny and new. Heroin became his solace and he lost himself in it.

Jerry sipped some tea. I asked him what happened to the collective.

It was the end. They all moved away. Michael's death was too much for them to get over. Most of them didn't survive. HIV is so cruel. It is cruel.

Jerry's hand was on the table. I put my hand on Jerry's hand and he looked at me.

I hate the world I have brought you to. You are young you should be living.

I choose to be here, I said to Jerry, I choose to be with you. I love you Jerry. I love you.

It was the first time I had said I love you and meant it. I was 19 what did I know. I knew.

Jerry was staring at me and Jerry started crying. I started crying my hand still on his hand I did not care who saw I did not care what they thought.

I said to Jerry, You have got to stop apologizing you have got to stop with this guilt. I am not a child I make my own choices you have got to hear, I did not ever believe I would live a life and I am now living a life and I am living a life because of you.

Jerry was looking at me Jerry said, I love, and then Jerry looked down Jerry paused. Jerry looked up again, Jerry said, I find those words difficult, I am sorry, I know those words should not be difficult. It is my upbringing, it is what I escaped from in my upbringing, it is my freedom, I have feared losing my freedom, in the past, and so I have fled from love, from declaring love, I did not need to declare love. But now I need to declare love, I want to declare love. I will try to say those words. I love you, John. You have changed me. I love you.

It is OK, Jerry, it is OK, I know, I said, I understand. And I felt ashamed, my neediness, my need to be told something when I was already being shown everything, I did not need him to say the words, his love was expressed in all else, in his home, in his conversation, in his food, in his way of being.

Shall we go, said Jerry, and so we stood from those plastic chairs stuck to the plastic table, I took our cups to the counter, my plate, thank you, I said, the owner nodded, flicked their eyebrows, said nothing, didn't need to say anything. It was dark, there was no one in sight, no traffic, or if there was I didn't see it, Jerry linked his arm into mine pulled me close, how lucky am I, Jerry said, this handsome young man on my arm, what a time to be alive.

I looked at him and I smiled but my instinct was to not look at him my instinct was to keep watch and quickly I switched to keeping watch because we were not safe. My arm was stiff my arm did not relent I had said I loved him but my arm did not relent. There was someone in the distance someone anyone and Jerry slipped his arm out of my arm and we edged away from each other we both did it and we kept it that way, just two men walking, barely saying anything until we were both safe in our home.

Bitter leaves. A pot of beans. Some of the tomato sauce from summer's crop. Should be enough till deep into spring. Made some bread yesterday. Couple of slices under the grill. Really it's beans on toast.

Candles lit. A record on. Nina, *Baltimore*. On the couch. This couch will probably last beyond me. Substantial as some earth. Will anyone want it when I'm gone. This sofa, that chair, our bed. They should be in the museum. Not here with me spilling food on them. Friend of a friend got me in touch with someone at the museum. Runs the national collection. Twentieth-century design. Sent photos. Wrote him everything Jerry had told me, everything I knew. Sent the message. Heard nothing. Heard nothing. Asked the friend, the friend's friend said the curator was snowed under, friend's friend was sure I'd hear soon. Eventually got a message from the curator's assistant. *Thank you so much for your message, and your interest in the twentieth-century collection. As you can imagine, we are inundated with offers of items that could join the collection, and we have very limited space. For this reason, we are unfortunately unable to accept your offer, but we once again thank you for your interest.*

That's all it said. Words like that. Never heard anything more from the friend of a friend. We never talked about it. Like they were embarrassed for me. About me. Like I should just go away. No one wants the furniture, no one wants it preserved, who wants that history preserved, the history that no one knows, the history that no one talks about, and so the work isn't preserved, and then the history can never be told, the story of these humans, trying to do something new, trying to be other than the norm, what ends up being preserved is the norm. What do I know, why would anyone care, this sofa, this chair, these lives, all gone. Beans, toast, bitter leaves, more light.

7

Jerry said he'd not seen a doctor for three years but then he needed to see a doctor and then things went fast. Jerry was tired sometimes then he was tired often, he'd sweat at night, he'd wake up drenched, here we go, he would say, I'm going.

It happened fast. Jerry's temperature shot up. All night he sweated. Sweated through sheets, sweated through T-shirts. Sleep was hard. He said I should sleep downstairs, try getting some sleep, but I couldn't sleep, I was so worried, I was listening out for him, came back to bed three am, wanted to be with him, went to his GP, the GP said, let's monitor your condition. The GP said, let me know if you don't get any better.

Jerry did not get any better, another night of sweat, temperature high, Jerry could barely eat, he didn't want to, couldn't, just drank mint tea, that was all, then another night, worse, I remember at dawn saying, we should go to the doctor, Jerry said, I do not want to see that man, he wants me dead. Jerry said, I want to go to the clinic.

We had no money on us, couldn't afford a cab. Waited until eight thirty to call Gareth, seemed an OK time to call, seemed rude to call before, what were we doing, anxious about what was rude. Jerry said, don't call yet, wait till eight thirty, don't want to be rude. Gareth answered straight away, Gareth said, how is he, Gareth said, No. Gareth said, I'll be there in thirty minutes.

Jerry was weak, could hardly walk. Jerry had a temperature, Jerry was freezing. Got Jerry dressed, got Jerry downstairs, Jerry sat on the sofa, put a blanket around Jerry, looked out onto his garden, he said, dormant, that's all Jerry said. There was a knock at the door, it was Gareth.

We got Jerry in the car, sat him in the front, I sat behind, my hand on Jerry's shoulder. Gareth drove and Gareth was a terrible driver, was proud of it, fast and relentless, Jerry winced and Jerry said, Gareth, please, can we go slower, please, I can't take it.

Gareth went slower, Jerry still winced, Jerry was still in pain, it was not Gareth's driving that made him hurt it was just being. We got stuck in traffic it took for ever what is for ever. Jerry didn't drive, I didn't drive, still can't drive, why drive.

It took for ever and we got there. Gareth said, let me know what time you want picking up and I said sure and we both looked at each other like, we might not need picking up.

We were at the clinic it specialized in HIV anyone could get an appointment it was where Jerry wanted to go. Jerry was weak but Jerry was still Jerry in the room where we waited there were men who were no longer themselves I had not known them did not know them would never know them but they were no longer themselves, they had been someone else, someone other before this, they should still be someone else, this parallel universe that should not be this universe, they should not be here, we should not be here.

We waited for ever we held hands Jerry was still Jerry. We waited for ever and they called Jerry's name. We went in a room and we sat down and the doctor asked questions and the doctor listened and the doctor said OK let me see and it was so quick it happened so quickly the doctor said, I think it's wisest if we admit you.

Jerry breathed out sharply, Jerry said he was scared and then Jerry said actually, he was relieved. And in that nanosecond he had decided for it to be OK because what else could he do. I was scared and I was scared. I felt like a child. Often with Jerry I no longer felt like a child but right then I felt like a child. Jerry was put in a wheelchair, Jerry had a look on his face like a kid, he had glee on his face he was in a wheelchair. They took Jerry for an X-ray they took Jerry for tests they said, visiting hours start at four, come back then.

Grim wild alone, out of the hospital, I did not know where I was, no money, or barely any, a few pounds, I could try and draw out more but I was at my limit and I could not go over my limit. I was meant to be in college, a lecture I would have slept in, a seminar that was meant to be registered but no one signed in, no one would miss me, no one cared.

I had three hours. No point in travelling home, no point in going to college, no point. I wandered. Down the hill, a memorial to who knows who, no one about, buses stuck, traffic stuck, unable to turn, a log jam, the memorial to who knows who in the way, what does it mean when they are in the way and not at peace. Sign for the heath. I followed it.

I knew all about the heath, I knew all that went on there, how glorious, how wild, how free, the fucking, the pleasure, I had never been there, it scared me, I did not understand its ways, its wildness, I did not understand how to be, how to make anything happen, I had such fear, when of course there was nothing to understand, it was beyond understanding, I walked onto the heath, grim, wild, alone.

Path lined with trees, bare, wildness above, strict below. Houses for rich people, no one there, left these behind, ponds, swimming steps, ropes across the water, no one swimming, past the pond, mud that used to be grass, now mud from thousands of relentless feet, no one there that day, abrupt hard hill up and suddenly the top, suddenly everything, as if everything can be seen, the whole city, or so it appeared, all laid out below. I tried to understand it, tried to find our home, tried to find the tower by us, the tower so vast when you are by it, a blur from here, I could not see our home, the whole city was meant to be our home, it was not our home.

It repelled me. I turned and walked into the heath, off the path, onto the grass, I did not want order I did not want it. A clearing, tree at its high point, benches around it, focused on the tree, stared at the tree, tried to imagine its roots, tried to understand its scope its balance its capacity. I was thinking about Jerry. Other trees over there, spindly, higher than sense, a nest up high, nest that shouldn't be there, but it is there, for them that is safety.

All is colour and I saw no colour. I did not know where to go. I sat on a bench. Someone was trying to fly a kite, the kite had no desire to be flown, it was in the air it was going nowhere why bother.

Stood and walked, downhill, deeper, trees, thickets, was this where I would go, was this where I wouldn't need to understand, it was so grim, what time was it, half one, no one was there, why would they be there, maybe men had been there twelve thirteen fourteen hours before, in the night, maybe they would be here again soon, Jerry said he was a child of the heath, when he was younger, before all of this, when life could be about possibility, before all possibility was eradicated, how was Jerry, how long did he have, please not now please give us more. I remember thinking this, thinking this to no one, asking please to no one, asking please to myself. I needed to piss, went deep into the scrub, trying to find a tree thick enough to hide me, hide me from no one, condoms on the ground, a cluster of them, left here, declaring this land, what this land was for, this land was for fucking. I pissed, I had been desperate to piss, my piss pouring down by the condoms, seeping into the condoms, my fluid with their fluid, whoever's fluid, who knew. The release. I was hungry, I needed food, not eaten all day, Jerry would be mad, he always said, you must eat, always. I headed back down, back from the grim, the wild, the alone.

Found a café. Got some toast. All I could afford. Time passed. I was used to time passing. I came from nowhere, time passing was a childhood occupation. How was Jerry, this man I'd not even known sixteen months before, this man who was now my everything, sixteen months, now it seems like nothing, then, years could happen in a week, everything was consequential, everything mattered, sixteen months with Jerry was bedrock, I was not myself before those sixteen months with Jerry, those sixteen months with Jerry were everything, I wanted more I wanted more, I wanted Jerry to live, but Jerry would die, we knew Jerry would die, Jerry knew he would die, Jerry had known for years, he had known, he knew.

Someone came into the café and all I could see were

flowers, flowers trapped in plastic, flowers that did not exist, as plastic as the plastic that encased them, and I realized, that is what I'm supposed to do, I am supposed to take flowers, but Jerry hated flowers, or at least he hated cut flowers, flowers forced to grow, flowers that had never lived, no real life, hated them for the plastic they were wrapped in, waste, all waste, that's what Jerry said, someone sent him flowers a couple of weeks before, someone trying to show him sympathy, someone trying to lift spirits, wish they hadn't, was what Jerry had said, roses sent when roses were not meant to grow, give them to next door, said Jerry, when I look at them all I think about is everything that is wrong.

What was I meant to do how was I meant to be. We had talked and talked and talked about how to feel, how to say what we felt, how to be honest, Jerry told me and told me I mustn't keep my feelings to myself, I mustn't hide them, even if I didn't understand them, even if I couldn't articulate them, we're in uncharted waters, he would say, we're pushed out far from shore, I cannot tell you what will happen I cannot tell you how I'm going to be it will get rough you have to be able to talk to me you have to be able to tell me how you feel.

He said this so much it was like I was the one dying. He said he would understand if it was too much for me, that I could leave him, that I was young, I should be living, I said to him, I am living.

But this was new this was unknown it wasn't just us it was happening to we were angry we were scared I was terrified we were exhausted and in it Jerry had grace. How was I meant to be what was I meant to do.

I left the café, I was on the high street, no one else on the high street, the high street deserted, or at least it seemed to me, the great big swell of nobody. A shop had postcards outside, postcards of the heath, postcards of art, postcards of illustrations, one was of an eye, elaborately drawn, the eye intense, pale blue, lines swirling off from the eye, nourishment from what the eye saw, Jerry loved eyes, I loved eyes, I bought the postcard. I asked in the shop if I could borrow a pen, I wrote on the postcard in big letters, decorative letters, proud letters,

TO MY JERRY
I LOVE YOU
ALWAYS YOURS
JOHN

I'd never written anything like it before. Anything with actual feeling. There was a post office, I bought a stamp, still in time for it to get to Jerry the next day, I addressed it, I sent it, that was that, so began our postcards, so began our paper trail.

It was almost visiting time I wanted to be there when the doors opened I wanted to be there with Jerry. There was a fruit stall, full, abundant, no one buying anything, on the pavement a box of daffodils, sign said '50p a bunch', many still in bud, tight skin holding flower in, whoever's stall it was saw me looking, they're local son, said the market stall holder, not many bother, said the market stall holder, the market stall holder said no more. Jerry loved daffodils, these daffodils were just like the daffodils pushing up through Jerry's soil through Jerry's garden, our garden, now my garden. I had one pound thirty left. I bought two bunches.

I got to the hospital I got to the ward I could not find Jerry I found Jerry. Hello my love said Jerry and I went to Jerry and I kissed him I did not care who saw I did not care who was in the other beds I did not care what anyone thought I kissed him. I gave Jerry the daffodils. Jerry laughed. I said are these allowed. He said, because they are from you they are.

Jerry said he was OK, Jerry said he'd been X-rayed, Jerry said they'd taken blood, his temperature was the same, he felt awful, he felt better for being admitted, everyone has been lovely, Jerry said, it's like a holiday camp.

Jerry was smiling I knew Jerry's smiles Jerry was smiling to say I'm OK are you OK.

He asked what I'd done with my day, I said I'd been on the heath, chip off the old block, he said. He started to cough it was violent, turn your back a minute, he managed to say, I turned my back, he was violent. I turned back, Jerry's hand was on my thigh, he looked tired, he looked pale, he looked unwell, I tried to not let my eyes show what I knew. Jerry knew.

Are you going to be OK, I said to Jerry. His teeth had been showing in his smile but his lips closed over them. He still smiled but his lips were closed. I'll be OK, said Jerry, knowing he wouldn't be OK. This is time passed in hospital, in the ward, we talked by not talking, by not saying and therefore saying, nothing like how we talked in the world, in our garden, in our home, over food, on our walks, that talk could not happen any more, not here, it couldn't, it wouldn't, we talked in a new way, by looks, by expression, by saying and not saying, that is all, that is how we could be.

Ready for some more checks, Mr Field. It was a nurse. Of course my dear, said Jerry, and Jerry smiled. I'd like you to meet my partner, this is John.

I smiled at the nurse, stayed sitting where I was, Jerry's hand on my thigh, the nurses look shifted from Jerry to me to Jerry to me to Jerry then to me and she said to me, you've got yourself a handful with this one. She put a thermometer in Jerry's mouth, felt Jerry's pulse, said to Jerry, do you feel able to walk or would you like a chair.

I would be most grateful for a chair, said Jerry.

Got me running rings already, said the nurse. I'll be back soon.

I played grown-up. Got a vase, got water, arranged the daffodils, took the shells from my pocket, I put them on the side, what was there to arrange, there was nothing, everyone else playing grown-up just as much as me, the nurse came back, said to Jerry but really said to me, these tests may take a while so visiting time may well be over by the time you're back.

I was helping Jerry into the wheelchair, thank you my love, he said, I never knew I'd ever have anyone who said my love to me freely, that I would be able to say my love so freely, I loved Jerry, I love Jerry.

I'll see you tomorrow, I said to Jerry. I'll come after college. I'll call everyone tonight. Can I bring anything for you? I'll call you in the morning. Will you be OK? I am here with you, always.

All this as he was wheeled away, Jerry's answers calming me, Jerry calming me, I love you and I'll see you tomorrow said Jerry. Then the nurse pushed Jerry through some doors and Jerry was gone.

There was nothing for me to do there, I was in the way, physically, psychologically, I remember the feeling, you are in the way. I pushed through doors, through doors, out.

Dark out. Not enough money to get home. No map on me. Jerry was my map. I relied on Jerry. I didn't know where I was, I turned right, I walked.

There were shops then there were no shops. Terrace of houses, comfortable, removed, endless line, behind them a train went by, this is the right course, east. The certainty of these homes was alien to me, would this ever be our life, Jerry and I, it would never be our life, what was our life, I loved our life, I was scared for our life, I was going to lose our life, our life was all I knew. Lights in houses, no one in them. In one window an old man, sat at a table, waiting for dinner, or just waiting, an old man, old, the old man looked younger than Jerry. Paths to the houses a patchwork, some diamonds of black and white, order in decoration, some a swirl, the grandeur, the street all terrace, paths abrupt next to each other, one decorated, next door a refusal, concrete, grit, who was better, who loved harder, decoration a cover for emptiness.

No one on the street in this darkness, I had been mugged once on a street like this, but I did not feel fear, I felt intensity, intensity of what I did not know, which is to say it was an intensity of love and not knowing what to do with that love, love that felt useless. A school, football pitch empty, a football left outside of touch, outside of play.

Joined up with a main road, no road sign, turned left, keep east, under a rail bridge, a road that wanted no walkers, I walked, hill rising, no hill where we lived, must be far from where we live, I wanted to be at home, I wanted Jerry.

Social housing on the left, a building sloped, diagonal side, balconies, space, garden neat, buildings all different, another with spiral staircase of concrete, each step floating free, tallest building frosted glass curved stairwells, long verticals of concrete holding frosted glass, long lines down, perspectives, what the eye needs to see, all eyes, not just the eyes of the wealthy, a main road, a crossroads, where should I go. Not north, that is clear, I know which way is north, due east the road suddenly small, the houses suddenly a village, I had no choice, I turned south. Barren street, a street no one cared for, a street that cars sped to pass through, I sped up, I didn't want to be there, cars sped north, they wanted out, their choice, let them go.

The road began to curve, did not want to go back on myself, train tracks came below and went off to the left, a road went with them, skirt around the edge, that's the way, I took that road. What would Jerry be doing, how was his test, what would his test show, is he dying, when will he die, will he feel safe will he feel loved will he sleep.

Take the road, the train tracks soon veer off right, inwards, eastwards, is this the right road, the road banks steep quick like it has purpose, top of the hill suddenly it stops, the road gives up, no signs, no direction, left or right, clearly right, keep veering, a street on the brink, signs for a prison, then signs for another prison, a land of prisons, city in another world, I was uneasy, I was not safe, I was not meant to be there, how else was I to get home, should I have called Gareth, I didn't want to call Gareth, didn't want to ask too much, we were going to need Gareth, we didn't know what was going to happen but we were going to need Gareth, how should Jerry be now, forties were so old to me then, seemed so old until I met Jerry, then I saw forties as possibility, forties should be possibility, should be threshold, should be beginning, that was how Jerry should be, why was this happening who was responsible who was killing Jerry. The road kept going I had no other road to take I kept going on the road. Barren land, crown of the hill, brutal barren block, council estate on the edge, unlovable, unloved, crest on top of the block, crest of the corporation of the city, crest as if the block below was a prison, its residents incarcerated, no joy, the block sentry over the city, the city all below it, doomed watch, the city before me, the flat low lands, this was in the right direction, I should not have been there, the wrong you go through to get to right, as if wrong or right were anything any more or were ever, Jerry was dying, there was no right, the hill relented, the road downward, warehouses with nothing in them, café that was closed, pub with no light, so dark, so horrible, was this our city, a street went off to the right, towards civilization, houses as refuge, but that was not my way, so dark, the edge of this world, I had to keep going on.

The road fell, a deep fall, a twist, hard down, no streetlights, all darkness, alone.

A dip as if the earth had been scoured out. Under a bridge then the road rose tight and twisted and trapped by walls, two brick walls, either side, tight, higher than my head, I could not see over, pavement tight to the wall, no cars, ahead the road took an abrupt turn, all I could see were road and pavement and wall and streetlights and what was meant to be sky, was it sky? A nightmare, a city. The city was there and it was not there. Was this even a road. I kept on. The turn came and it curved and it curved, revealing nothing, an endless loop of road, all I would ever see again was this road, and then it relented, the walls relented, a tube station ahead, it was OK, it was OK, I was somewhere, but then I got closer, the tube station was abandoned, closed, fenced off, shuttered, no one here, I had to keep going, to the right of the road wasteland, barren scrub, wasteland the size of a town, stretching to no end, Jerry would have loved it, did he know it, a city of wasteland in this city, train tracks cutting through, converging, it hit me, this was the wasteland I saw every time I'd come to the city from my family home, before the city became my home, before Jerry became my family, I would be on the train and it would almost be at the station but it would pause, always, in this wasteland, waiting to enter the city, like you had to ready yourself to enter, purge yourself, of all you are leaving behind before you enter, rid yourself of it, purge yourself in this wasteland and then in you can come.

Warehouses ahead, a complex, there were people, who were these people, chaos, they looked like me, my age, barely out of adolescence desperate to be adult, to belong, they were a world away, they had life, streaming toward a track off the road, spotlights at the end of it, Jerry had told me about it, he knew them, a party after after after hours, the evening after the day after the night before, when hours were redundant, when all that matters is the party, they were going there now, but not me, this was not me now, my people and not my people, I knew no one, I needed Jerry, another world, I wanted to be them so bad, to be going their way, where nothing mattered and so everything mattered, that wildness, that release, out here where no one cares, I wanted that wildness, I wanted that wildness with Jerry. I wanted to be home, I wanted Jerry home, I wanted Jerry.

    Walked on, over a canal, redundant, a garage on the corner, forecourt lit as welcome, no cars to be welcomed, only kids, kids pouring in, I poured in with them, wanted to be with them, just for a minute, my age, my equivalent, they could be me, I could be them, what were they buying, fags, chewing gum, bottle of water, all they needed, I was so thirsty, I'd been walking for ever, I dug out all the coins I had, stood in the corner of the garage, all these versions of me pouring through, getting all they needed, me a version of them, same but separate, I had just enough, coins cobbled together, little carton of orange from the fridge, joined the queue of versions of me, it was like I was them, for a moment, I paid for the drink, headed for the door, onto the forecourt, it was like I was them, for a moment, they peeled off left, I went right, they were versions of me again, not me.

    The train station was before me, the place of my arrival, the place that birthed me into the city. Before, the endless brick wall that lined its tracks, sex workers with no chance of getting work, sexless sex shops, I knew where I was, it was my city again, I had taken this route before, I had taken this route. It was another forty minutes and then I was home, keys in the door, door shut. Jerry's air, my air, and then I realized. It would be my first time sleeping without Jerry first time in our home alone and that this would be my life soon and this was all there was and I fell on the sofa and I cried and I cried and I cried.

8

Summer. The scaffold is up the outline of the tower it is there it is real it will happen. This is the last summer I do not know what I will do.

That summer Jerry got better, better meaning not dead, he said, and he said it looking at me daring, daring me to laugh daring me to not laugh. He was out of hospital he was as if normal in our world of nothing normal. It was like Jerry was well, well enough to go about living, well enough to not need constant care, well enough to often not need any care. We lived life as if all was OK for as long as we could live life as if all was OK. What else could we do we lived we had to live.

We were happy, happy meaning alive, happy meaning in love, happy meaning terrified. Happy meaning day to day, happy meaning simplicity, happy meaning anger. Jerry had energy we did things. Jerry had no energy we did nothing, we stayed home, I held him, we talked, he held me, skin disappeared, I was him, he was me, that's how it was. More than merging, a sameness. Doors open, honeysuckle night air, the sameness, the strangeness, life with Jerry still strange to me, alien, in another man's home, me trying to be an adult, what did I know then, that I loved Jerry, that is all I knew.

I had graduated, I was broke, needed a job. There's the Albion, said Jerry, try there.

By that Saturday I had my first shift at the Albion, collecting glasses, chaos, unhinged, furtive wild mass, overspill on the street, some of them never even going inside, they bought cans of beer cheap down the road, hid in the overspill, the pavement only for overspill no one could pass by, the pavement blocked all night with overspill, not that there was anyone around to use the pavement, no one else around all night, only those of us going to the Albion, to play, to work, to work there was to play, broken paradise, said Jerry, three minutes from our door. That's how close it was, three minutes, up through the estate, onto the main road, the main road with no purpose, the Albion had not been bombed, all around it had been bombed, wasteland, devastation, blocks built behind it, estates, our estate, another estate built eleven years later, no hope, idealist, bleak the day it opened, we pissed on it, all of us, the overspill used it as a urinal, somewhere to piss on the way home, or when you'd just arrived, or whenever, such disdain, the estate a sewer, my shift was collecting glasses, my shift was bringing them back to the bar, my shift was washing glasses, my shift was putting fresh glasses out ready. My shift was being cheeky my shift was stripping off my top my shift was flirting my shift was being groped my shift was groping my shift was doing shots my shift was doing speed my shift was turning straight boys my shift was sucking cock in the gents my shift was sucking cock in the dark room my shift was dancing my shift was screeching everyone was screeching, hours of screeching, fucking about, this was work, when Jerry was well enough Jerry came with me, propped up at the end of the bar, safe in the chaos, witness to it, central to it and safe, Paul by his side most of the time, Paul the landlord, Paul who allowed all this to happen, the Albion had been straight, the previous landlord a crook, no one went near it, get your lights punched out if you did, as soon as the straights left the violence sucked out of it, but the tension remained, this place kinetic, a bar made for trouble, the place open till three weeknights, four on weekends, break from time break from law, lawlessness allowed, no one else around, no one cared, police knew what we were doing, there was no more violence so why should they care about a bunch of queens ruining themselves. No one complained, no one gave a shit what we were up to, I was 21 when I started, it was everything.

Whenever Jerry came to the Albion I would look over he would have that look in his eyes, glee, joy, militancy, terror, resignation, resignation that all was lost, lost for everyone in the room, it would not last, nothing good would last, but it was here and it was now we have to live it. Atoms and molecules came together formed Jerry they would disperse same with all of us here this was fleeting why fake permanence why pretend otherwise. Jerry's favourite night was Thursday night, music to make this sad old queen happy, he'd say, records from when he was young, 'Menergy', 'I'm So Hot For You', 'Love Pains', 'So Many Men' so many of the songs sad happy, bitterness and regret and loss and hope and belief and love, and sex, yearning for sex, hunting for sex, fucking, getting fucked, obsessed with getting fucked, regretting getting fucked, wanting it more and more and more. Self-belief, self-realization, determination, 'Passion', 'Megatron Man', 'Handsome Man', 'Right On Target', 'I'm A Man', 'I'm Coming Out', 'Tell You', 'Body Strong', what was this world, felt like freedom, gnarled and twisted, why should freedom mean purity.

    Thursday nights, men out on their own, after work, one more drink after drinks, closing time everywhere else, the Albion only just beginning, popping their head round the door, hopeful, on their own, no pressure, a mass of them, all of them popping their head round the door, no pressure, turning up and finding that it's on, that it's happening, like they hoped it would be, each of them playing their part in it being on, everything active, they all made the party, it's everything, everything they needed in this dump, this hovel, no one pretended otherwise, why pretend, what mattered was the energy, the possibility, the decision to be present, to show up, what else are you going to do, what else can you do? Straight lads from the estate dealing, straight lads from the estate trade, straight lads from the estate 'straight', pleasure was pleasure. There was always this moment when the mass became the mass, before that moment seemingly disparate people, but then they became the mass, unleashed, from then on till the end of the night I was out on the floor in the wild in the swirl intense, stacking up glasses taking glasses back to the bar then I'd go back out again, it's all I did, I loved it, constant contact, constant connection, all these men, some wanting me some wanting others, I didn't care, I loved to see it happen, to watch it unfold, it always happened, two guys just met at the beginning, they'd be laughing touching letting each other know after a couple of pints but still not knowing, it could still not happen, it was always going to happen, another pint a shot they'd be dancing if you could call it dancing, falling all over each other, the swirl all around, the same story playing out all around, I was witness to it, night after night, every night this energy, the energy endless, I could watch it and watch it and be in it and be in it, till the lights went up and whoever was left would have to decide who was going back to whose, sometimes the decision was easy, one of them had their own place, one of them had more beer in the fridge, one of them had more drugs in the drawer, sometimes they had to work it out, where to spend that night, they knew they'd spend that night together, that's all that mattered, nothing more. I'd get picked up sometimes, but when the lights went up I still had to work, still had to tidy, most couldn't be bothered to hang around and wait, some waited, we'd always go back to theirs, never Jerry's, that was our rule, we never brought anyone else back home. Anyway there was the darkroom there were the toilets I got what I needed at the Albion, why would I need anything else. I got the education I needed, the education I desired, social education, community education, energy education, the Albion was my everything, college became irrelevant to me, I'd worked out how to do the bare minimum at college, worked out how I could pass by barely being there, college didn't care they'd had no idea I existed. I got my degree but who cares in the end I didn't need college Jerry was my college the Albion was my college it was all I needed.

It was all how Paul intended, he set the Albion up that way, LOVE, LIFE AND LIBERTY was painted on the wall, a map of the world next to it, drinks were cheap the beer was terrible the hangovers the worst it was all part of it. Waifs and strays were given work if someone didn't have a home if someone was kicked out of their home Paul would find them space upstairs, give them a bed, or if upstairs was full he'd find them space somewhere else, they could live rent free if they just did some shifts, everyone stole from the till all the time everyone stole drinks all the time staff dealt from behind the bar all the time Paul knew Paul didn't care, it was what it took to make the place be what it was, it couldn't have been any other way. This was how you made community this is how you make community it is messy and it is alive.

About ten months after I started, maybe eleven, Paul gave me some posters, told me to put them up.

29th CHAPTER
ACTION PLANNING
GATHER AT THE ALBION
7pm TUESDAY 28th JUNE

Tell Jerry, Paul said. See if he's got the strength.

He's doing good right now, I said to Paul.

I mean mental strength, said Paul.

I told Jerry the next day and he laughed and he put his hand to his forehead and Jerry said, what else are we going to do.

Jerry was looking older, his skin, his eyes, he knew it, he'd see himself in the mirror and say, who's that sad sack.

Have you ever protested before, Jerry said to me that morning, maybe it was afternoon.

I never had, I told him so.

Would you like to pop your cherry. It'll be drama.

But when I asked him about it the next day and the next day he'd say, maybe we won't go, and then, not putting myself through that bullshit again and, all that aggro, all that energy wasted, all that division, I'm so tired of it, and then, did Paul mention Graham, and then, maybe he won't come, and then,

I'm definitely not going, and then, a couple of hours before, let's go.

We got to the Albion 6.59pm, it was busy already, good to see you Jerry, someone said, happy you're here Jerry, said someone else, but then someone else didn't say hello to Jerry, someone else caught Jerry's eye stared at Jerry then averted their eye, I saw. Jerry didn't care Jerry carried on acting oblivious, where shall we sit, he said, ah yes over here.

What's the headcount, someone said, thirty-seven? OK good. Let's call the meeting to order, my name is Graham Forbes, for anyone who doesn't know me I'm the chair of this chapter. I understand there was another attempt to unseat me but since they once again failed to file the motion in time the meeting will continue without another election vote. We will start this meeting as we begin all meetings with a minute's silence for our comrades, friends, lovers and allies whose lives have been lost since we last met. David Hatherley. George Hall. Bambini. Tracy Sargent. Terry Holmes.

The list continued, so many names, and then the names stopped and there was silence. Jerry was crying I could feel his body shake against mine, I put my arm around Jerry I held Jerry. Someone clapped and then everyone clapped, Jerry clapped, still crying, everyone clapped and they clapped, on and on and then they stopped.

Our next action will be on July 27th, said Graham. It will be at the Annual General Meeting of Evengate to protest against their continuing refusal to share knowledge about treatments that could prolong or even save the lives of those living with HIV. Does anyone have any objections or points to make about the proposed ac

On whose authority are you making those plans, came a voice from the back, you have no authority in this room.

Here we go, said Jerry in my ear, and some clapped and some groaned and Jerry did neither, it went on, I couldn't follow it, the meeting took two hours or two days or two years to decide nothing about what could have been a disagreement lasting twenty minutes, we are all exhausted, said Graham eventually, Paul was circling, he needed the meeting to end, the chairs cleared away, punters would be turning up soon, even on a Tuesday evening they'd come, they wanted to drink they wanted to dance they wanted to forget, the meeting was meant to be finished at nine it was 9.07, I was due on my shift, I was nodding off, no one was satisfied no one was engaged everyone was despairing what else could they do but despair.

We are all exhausted, said Graham, none of us want to be here. This should not be our lives. I am asking you once again to put your life on the line, because what else are we going to do. We know there is research we know there are results we know there is knowledge if we do not demand to know it they will never tell us and not only will we die but those ahead of us will also die. And we can stop that now. Who is with me? We can stop that now.

The meeting resolved to have another meeting. A couple of weeks later, plans were made, action cells formed, cells that worked independently, if one cell was stopped, other cells would continue, a wave of actions all at once, I'll do what I can, Jerry said, even if you are just there it is enough, said Graham, the two were talking again, I did not see how it happened but it happened, I asked Jerry about it once and he said, divas always command the stage.

I got co-opted into the core cell. Graham said, we need someone young and innocent, and all eyes were on me. They had a contact at the venue, they could get three of us temp jobs at the venue, meet and greet, show people to their seats, be there and be invisible, we had to look like we could be an usher, I looked like I could be an usher.

You will be helping speakers with the microphone, with moving the podium, which means you will have the chance to take over the microphone, you can take over the AGM.

Graham was looking at me like I had a choice but that I also had no choice. What about Jerry, I said to Graham, we'll look after Jerry, said Graham, she always lands on her feet.

Nine days before the AGM, the contact at the venue got me working straight away so I could be natural. I had no suit so I got a suit from a charity shop, it did nothing for me which is what we needed it to do, I needed to look nothing, obliging, dutiful, irrelevant. I never met the contact she was leaving anyway she didn't care, but we covered our tracks, no one would know, I was just some short-term hired help. I did a shift at a conference on the steel industry I sucked a delegate off from the conference on the steel industry, in the toilets, he wanted to fuck me in the toilets, I said no, he wanted to cum in my mouth, I said no, he came on my face I wiped it off but didn't see some went on my jacket and so I spent the rest of the conference greeting delegates from the conference with the residue of a delegate from the conference's cum on my jacket. There was a conference on international tourism too I didn't suck anyone off I mean what is this place.

In the evenings we prepared a speech for me, worked out

what I could say, what would have impact if I only got two seconds on the microphone, what would have impact if I got ten seconds on the microphone, what would have impact if I made it to a whole minute, they prepared me, the young and the innocent and the dutiful and the irrelevant.

The day came I was terrified I set off early, had to be at the conference centre by seven thirty, even though we were planning my action for around two. When I left Jerry was still in bed, Gareth was going to look after Jerry, was going to take Jerry to the protest outside the venue, was going to protest with Jerry, was going to take Jerry home if he needed to go home. I was worried I wanted him to stay home I wanted him to stay away, I've done this a million times, said Jerry, don't worry about me.

I got to the conference centre, by now I knew the entrance, security on the entrance knew me, I knew where the lockers were where the toilets were I was a natural. We helped them set up their stage we helped them put up their posters and their banners we put agendas on every seat, the agendas said on the front of them *EVENGATE: ALWAYS TOMORROW* I put the agendas on the seats what the fuck do you think you're doing, someone from Evengate said to me, are you a fucking idiot, put them straight, this room is a fucking disgrace.

I did what I was told I was dutiful, irrelevant. Delegates started arriving at 9.30am and I was dutiful and irrelevant even when delegates were saying fucking faggots and if they die it's god's will, I smiled a smile of welcome and was silent and dutiful and irrelevant and I knew the protest outside was happening, it was working, I found out how it was going by what the arriving delegates said, how angry they looked, how traumatized, a die-in on the steps of the conference centre, fake blood poured over themselves, Jerry one of them, was Jerry OK I had no way of knowing, a delegate came in frantic, fake blood on his suit, I'M CON-TAMINATED, he was screaming, I'M CONTAMINATED, it was fake blood. I stayed dutiful and irrelevant and smiled and helped him clean him of fake blood helped him clean it all away.

When the AGM got started I was on stage most of the time dutiful and irrelevant, my role had been well rehearsed, moving the microphone, moving the podium, adding another microphone if there were two speakers, getting extra chairs, taking chairs away, invisible and irrelevant, I was good at what I did how could I not be it was easy, I did it well so no one was suspicious, our contact at the venue had lied about my experience, my experience was allegedly faultless, I had to live up to my lie, and so I was on stage when the next die-in happened, seven of them made it onto the stage, others lay down in the aisles, each with a freezer bag of fake blood, each of them fake blooded themselves, they started their chant,

> 2 4 6 8
> EVENGATE IS FILLED WITH HATE
> THEY HATE GAYS
> SO WE SAY
> THIS IS WHY WE'LL DIE FROM AIDS

They chanted it twice then one of them saw a chance and grabbed the microphone then lay back down again, now they were amplified, the crowd were booing, shouting, the chanting was so loud, some in the crowd tried to get out but they couldn't get out they were blocked by the die-in, the executive board left the stage, get them out now, someone was screaming at me, DO SOMETHING, I was acting shocked, I was acting scared and clueless and rooted to my spot, what were the other ushers doing what were the other ushers doing, not my responsibility mate, said another of the ushers when they were screamed at, they were a legit usher, or at least to me they were legit, maybe they were another cell, we're not security, said the other usher, it's not our remit, and so I followed their lead and did nothing and said nothing, just looked scared and appalled and also absolved of any responsibility, while inside I was screaming and screaming elated and terrified because it would be me next.

   The die-in dead were dragged off one by one Graham was one of them he caught my eye while he was chanting, dragged off by the arms but still chanting, a couple of photographers zooming in, they must have expected another boring AGM that no one nowhere would want photos from and now suddenly here was something happening, they could sell their photos, they took their photos, Graham caught my eye and his eyebrows flicked up and down and he kept on chanting and chanting and that was it.

   They gave me agency, they said to choose a time from two that felt right to me that I should choose my own moment. No pressure they said but my actions could alter the course of the epidemic. I was scared I didn't know how Jerry was I had no way of knowing how Jerry was, we shouldn't have agreed to do it we shouldn't have taken part.

   I had no clue what I was doing I was lost dejected alone, the AGM started up again, I was fulfilling my role again, could not see my chance, could not see the point, it was gone three, I was deflated, I had failed, I wasn't going to do it, and then the speaker on the stage, whoever they were, they came to their closing remarks,

On a personal note, the speaker said, and I must stress that I am talking now as an individual, and as a Christian, not in my capacity as research development director of Evengate, although I do believe I share these values with our founding family, I wanted to reflect on the events we have endured today at our AGM. I know that all God asks of those sinners who stormed the stage is to repent their sins and he shall offer them forgiveness. Their sins are many, the sin of their lifestyle, their un-Christian ways, living against the word of the Bible, but God's love is great and if they repent their sins, he shall forgive them. Whether this gay plague is a punishment handed down from God, we cannot tell, but we do know that homosexuality is a sin, and we only pray that they reject their depraved lifestyle, and that they stop harassing this great organization that was founded on true Christian values. Maybe if they repent their sins, and radically change their lifestyles, maybe the epidemic of which they speak will merely disappear. I know God will not grant them mercy until that day. I ask you to vote a resounding no on the amendment, in God's name. I thank you.

His name was Brian Doughty, it said so on my programme, how fucking dare he, some stood and clapped and cheered, everyone was talking, some on the executive board stood and clapped, others were in huddles, one stood and ran round and crouched between two colleagues, the AGM was off the rails for a moment again, this was my chance this was my time, how fucking dare he, I walked up to the microphone like I was supposed to do, I was due to move the microphone and the lectern to the side to allow the screen to be lowered, the next presentation had imagery, I walked up to the microphone only I did not move the microphone I took out of my suit pocket the speech we had prepared and I walked up to the microphone and I talked into it.

My name is Jonathan Grant and my partner Jerry will soon die from AIDS-related causes. We do not know when, but we do know he will die, unless companies such as Evengate begin to share their knowledge and research. To be clear, if you began to share your knowledge, you could save my partner Jerry's life.

I had made it to ten seconds, no one had stopped me, no one had switched off the microphone, I was crying, I couldn't talk I had to talk, I carried on reading, the photographers were in front of me I carried on reading.

We know that your knowledge and expertise could save the lives of millions. We know that your knowledge and expertise could lead to pioneering treatments. Isn't that the founding purpose of Evengate, to pioneer?

Still no one stopped me. What we had prepared wasn't what I needed to say. I looked up from my piece of paper and I just spoke,

I understand that many of you do not agree with the way I live my life. I am not asking for your agreement. From what I understand, you are here today to make money. Can you not see the clear benefit to your company, and to your shareholders, if you unlocked the potential in your research

I'd heard at least two of the speakers during the day use the term unlock the potential, it was the bullshit they liked. I was over thirty seconds, this was crazy, I heard something

I looked to the side security were coming across the stage I held the lectern I started shouting MY PARTNER IS DYING, HE IS DYING, JERRY WILL DIE

They were pulling me I had the lectern they yanked they pulled me to the floor the lectern fell a glass of water smashed, security picked me up under the arms I was howling I was screaming JERRY WILL DIE JERRY WILL DIE and they dragged me off and they dragged me out.

I was arrested I was put in a cop car I was taken to the police station I was put in a cell a couple of hours, we'd talked through what could happen I kept my cool it was OK it was OK do not freak out I had no one's number I couldn't call anyone who was I going to call my parents? And then I was given a caution I was released, it was seven past eight, something like that. The plan was to meet at Gigi's, so I headed to Gigi's, no idea who would be in Gigi's, how many, me still in my terrible suit, the suit of the irrelevant, that I never wanted to wear again in my life, I caught myself in a reflection and I looked so normal and I realized I am normal I am alive this is normal.

Got to Gigi's walked down the steps into Gigi's, pushed open the door of Gigi's it was rammed, everyone all around the piano, this tiny space that you can survey from the door, more steps down into Gigi's, everyone all arms around each other, everyone was singing, where was Jerry there was Jerry I could see him at the bar I waved and then someone saw me and that person shouted my name and someone else cheered I couldn't see who and then everyone was cheering and the pianist stopped and they stood and clapped it was Gigi out of drag, a Monday night why should they bother, Johnny someone shouted, but all I could see was Jerry and I started crying I was crying, through the crowd, people patted my shoulder people hugged me I thanked them I hugged them but I only wanted to get to Jerry here was Jerry my Jerry on a stool spritely as anything that smile those eyes my boy, he said in my ear, my love, and we kissed and kissed, it was my Jerry.

Gigi was playing the piano again, she was leading the song, the same song they'd been singing when I'd walked in, 'Tomorrow'.

I was crying, Jerry was crying, what did you do, said Jerry, what did you do.

I started to tell him and he said darling I know we were told every single moment every single word. I am so proud of you. How lucky am I to have you in my world.

I was crying Jerry was crying, I asked what happened to him, he said, oh it was a typical Monday really, I pretended to be dead which is not far from the truth anyway and then a nice young copper said to me I'm terribly sorry but I'm going to have to pick you up and put you in the back of my van and I said Jesus Lord the gates of heaven hath opened.

Jerry was OK no one had hurt him they looked after him his spirits were high.

Gigi was on another song, 'On The Street Where You Live'.

We stayed till Gigi kicked us out, all of us all night arm in arm singing top of our voices, full lungs, I have sung like that nowhere else, sung as if I could sing, can you play one for me Gigi, said Jerry, and Jerry went to Gigi's ear, everyone went quiet, then Gigi started playing and then Jerry smiled and he sang to me, those eyes on me, that smile, he sang 'Losing My Mind', and he sang and he sang and it's like he is still singing it to me today.

9

8.12am. They started work at 7.59. Saturday, they've been building what three weeks now, the board says the build will take ten months that really means over a year, over a year of this noise and then the light will be gone.

It is so hot I would open the door but for the drilling. Who's awake who's up. Let's scroll. No not him he's out of his mind. He is also out of his mind. Next one. They're needy. Him, he never answers. What about this guy, he's hot. Message him, hey. Probably out of his mind. Never mind. Let's get on with the day.

John Coltrane, *Lush Life*. Jerry's copy. I love morning I love this light, next year will be shadow. 'Like Someone In Love'. Let's make things. That's what Jerry would say. Let's make things. Start with a sauerkraut. Just started eating the last jar, will need more soon. Here's a cabbage slice the cabbage, slice it fine. Wait there's a message he's replied what does it say.

— You high?
Let's reply.

— making sauerkraut

Put the phone down, get the salt, two teaspoons. Have a look he's replied, three times

– ?
– Pervert
– Loser

Massage the cabbage, squeeze it out, wring it, massage it, make it juice. OK now leave it for a bit let it sit. I'd be his best fuck he'd had all year he wouldn't be mine. Loser.

Wonder if that guy's up, that guy who came round after his run, that's what I want, he was wild, let's find him, here he is, message him, you out running? Bet he won't be, cast the line out anyway, who knows.

Turn the record over. Back to the kraut, it's doing good, squeeze it again, squeeze it massage it press it down, then do it more, Jerry used to say, it's never enough. It's never enough! He'd say it for everything. Food drink sex work love friends energy life. It's never enough. Oh man what is that. Drilling. It's like it's underneath me. Make coffee. Oh wait there's a message. It's the running guy

– 6K

                                                   – not bad

– need to let off some steam

                                                       – I'll bet

– 15 mins?

                                                – I'll be ready

– Address again?

                                    – 1 Nova Scotia House

He's read it he's not replying he's on his way. OK what do I need to do. Clean out my arse, that's a given, that's easy, I'm so regular, no one cared so much before, maybe awkwardness before, didn't talk so much about sex before, now sex is in high definition, wide arsehole gaping, I'm into it, it's cool, I want to be ready for him, wait did I take my pill, I took my pill, as soon as I could get them I've been taking my pill, I never forget my pill, I always think, did I take my pill.

OK open the bathroom window OK that fucking drilling OK go downstairs light some incense OK put on a record, Patrick Cowley, what even am I wearing, trackpants, a sweatshirt, that's it, that's all I need, did I even brush my teeth, knock at the door, haha he's here.

Open the door he's laughing pushes the door open pushes me against the wall pushes the door shut he is on me, full body presses against me, mouth is on me mine in his, he's hard already, pushes it hard against me, his hand down the back of my trackpants already, he's rubbing my hole already, he pulls his head back for

Hello, he says,

Hello, I say, eyes all enveloping, he smells of moss, keeps his crotch pressed into me, leans back, unzips his windcheater, his hand back round my arse, I hitch myself lower, we fit I could be here for ever I could be here for ever, it's never enough, his heft, his force, his flesh. All of this flesh, his breath, his saliva, his and mine, put my hand on his chest, rub his nipples through his top, remember how he squirms then hardens when I play with his nipples, we remember what each other's bodies do, this is only the second time, we remember, he winces, he pulls his head away eyes shut lip held by teeth and then his eyes open again, and he smiles and then he pushes me down, I let him push me down, pushes his crotch in my face, running shorts over leggings, two layers between me and his cock, this is all part of it, the unveiling, the reveal, the before, the during, the after, pushing my face into his crotch, the smell is metal, my mouth open, rubs his cock under those two layers back and forth across my mouth, I'm looking up at him, he's looking down at me, I'm smiling, he's smiling, he puts his thumb in my mouth, he pulls his crotch away, it's just his thumb, my mouth, his gaze. He's holding my mouth open, he spits into my mouth the spit lands on my tongue, I close my mouth on his thumb I suck hard I tongue his thumb I pull down his shorts, it's time, I hitch myself up, his thumb out of my mouth, his hands onto the back of my head like he's guiding me. In his leggings his cock reaches almost to the side of his body. Burrow my nose into his crotch again, cold and hot, cold from the fabric, hot from the blood, there's a stain of precum I lick it, put my hands to his waistband and peel down and there it is there is the head of his cock, my hands go to his arse my mouth can do the rest, and first I brush it with my stubble and I am looking up at him, then I lick at it, first lick barely touching then I let my tongue stay longer, still looking up at him, now I'm looking just at his cock, I want him to see me looking just at his cock, he sees me looking just at his cock.

My memory of fucking is warped by fucking today I can't help it. A guy was sucking my cock I was three hours into my shift, I was at the Albion, we were in the toilets, in the cubicle. The guy said he was straight the guy said he didn't know what he was doing the guy said he didn't know why he was there, he knew what he was doing he knew why he was there. The guy said I was so pretty the guy said I was so young, the guy said he had a fantasy the guy said he'd always wanted to have a cock in his mouth and so what else was I going to do. I took him to the toilets and took him into a cubicle and he got on the floor and he unzipped my fly and got out my cock and he put it in his mouth, but really this is all he did he had no clue, put my cock in his mouth and was all moaning and groaning like I was the lucky one but really he was clueless and so I held the back of his head and fucked his face, what else was I going to do. He gagged and he choked, boo-hoo poor him. He had his cock out he was jerking his cock it was everything to him. His eyes were closed it wasn't me he was thinking of I was a conduit I didn't care. I was close I pulled out I jerked my cock I came on his face I came on his shirt he came all over his trousers oh fuck he said oh fuck he said about cumming he said about being covered in cum oh fuck he said again, maybe now his fantasy had been fulfilled, maybe now the acceptance maybe now the shame, maybe both, this was him, this was what he wanted, deal with it.

    He opened his eyes looked up at me, how was I, he said, I said, the dream. He stood and my cum was on his face, clean shaven but stubble pushing out, cum caught in it, I put my thumb to his face I wiped it I held my thumb there to let him know he was tagged. I had to work I opened the cubicle Barry was cleaning the toilets he saw me and he said hello dear, and he saw the guy and he said, you want some tissues.

    There were a few glasses left on the ledge around the room, not so many, it was easy, I loved the work, it was all the work I wanted, it was the world I wanted, Paul was in his spot, by the bar, how's Jerry, he said.

He's painting, I said, all the time. He is up early and he paints and he does his community work and he comes home and he paints. He cooks and he gardens and he paints. He likes me working here it means he's alone to paint, he says he can focus, he says he is trying to find the line.

I think we've lost her, said Paul, he was smiling at me, he winked.

I said, I get the feeling he's always been gone.

You know you're his first, said Paul. Before you he'd never lived with anybody he's never had a boyfriend he never had a partner you are his first.

I know, I said and I thought about it and I said, are we boring.

Jerry was here earlier watching them shoot some porn in the basement, said Paul, did he tell you.

I made a face like I was scandalized but I knew, Jerry told me he was going, I can get you a part if you like.

We were together we were free. My shift would finish 2am 3am 4am, depending on the day, depending on the day maybe I'd go back to some guys, maybe I'd go to the baths, the Coliseum, open 24 hours, it never closed, by some old train tracks, on the edge of the City, a nine-minute stumble from the Albion, a seven-minute stumble home, some treated it like a hotel, a couple of hours sleep on a sun lounger, sun loungers lined up in a neon-lit room with no windows, painting of a sunset on the walls, and grapevines, paintings of pillars, the ceiling painted blue sky with clouds, a pool, a few sometimes swam in it, why would you come here to swim.

That guy I'd face fucked, he disappeared, the shift was normal the shift was hilarious, I was drunk, when it was over

I wasn't done, I cleared up I did what I had to do, I stumbled out, my evening meal had been sambuca, I stumbled down the road round the corner, in nine minutes I was there, through the car park no one else around, pay up, got towels, into the locker room, strip, I was as swift as I could be, one towel round my waist, the other in the locker, for after, to dry myself, whenever after would be. The lockers a warren, past the entry to the bar, the graveyard, Jerry called it when he used to come, he'd not been with me for a while, old men on leather couches sleeping or passed out or unconscious, naked and inert, nothing happened there, past more lockers up stairs so thin, the first floor a warren of cabins, men loitering outside cabins, men inside cabins laid down arse in the air, asking for it from anyone, the sound of fucking from somewhere, not here, I went up one more flight, headed to the sauna, I liked to pretend it was an actual spa, got to the sauna opened the sauna door there was no one in the sauna, I sat in the sauna I opened my towel I leaned back my legs spread wide. A guy came into the sauna he was awful, he came and sat close to me he opened his towel I closed my towel sorry I'm not a charity. He sat there he played with himself he sat there he played with himself I looked at the ceiling. He was needy he was nervous he got the message he did up his towel he left quickly I hope he finds what he wants it's not me. I opened my towel again I played with myself I got myself hard it didn't take much. The door opened two guys came in they were laughing, both looked at me one really looked at me. They sat down they opened their towels they were talking they pulled their dicks out they rearranged themselves, I know mate I can't fucking believe it.

    Can you believe it, said the other.

I cannot.

Mate.

My presence stopped them or maybe they wanted to stop anyway, maybe they couldn't believe it, and that was it, what was their friendship I had no friends I had Jerry. The one who had really looked before was really looking, he played with his cock, absent minded with intention, lazy and loaded, the other one looked at the ceiling, the other one laughed to himself, the other one rubbed his eyes, the other one looked at me and looked at his friend, too fucking hot in here, he said, his excuse, he made his excuses, got up and left, his friend smiled at me, lazy turning less lazy, I was hard, he came over, sat right by me, his mouth on mine, it was on, he tasted rank, beer fags curry beer fags all of it, I bet I tasted rank, his hand on my cock mine on his, he was hairy, fleshy, just my type, tattoo on his bicep, anchor of a sailor, big, badly done, so startling then, a tattoo, he bent down, swallowed my cock in one go, gagging, he didn't care he made me out of my mind it was wild, he came up, spat his saliva on my cock, went all the way down again, I was usually the one sucking cock I was greedy, he came up and he kissed me I could taste my cock and he said come on I want you to fuck me, he stood he fastened his towel his dick was hard he pulled me up by the hand I fastened my towel my dick was hard, he went out I followed him what else could I do, he held my hand he led me he looked back he smiled, he slapped his own arse with his other hand, stairs, we were on the cabin floor, it stank, shit, who cares, men loitering, waiting, let them, TVs up high in corners, porn on the TVs, American porn, never the porn they shot in the basement of the Albion, fucking on the TV, no sound coming from the TV, the sound of fucking was real. He led me by the hand, he took condoms from a dispenser he took lube from a dispenser he took me by the hand. A cubicle, man on his own, finger in his arsehole, another cubicle, another man in it alone, slumped asleep maybe dead probably asleep. An empty cubicle wait it's the cubicle with an opening and bars into the next cubicle, a cubicle for voyeurs, didn't want to watch or be watched, another cubicle it's empty OK this one, in and lock the door, crash mattress black wide clean on a platform that was it that was the room he was on me, pulled off my towel and pulled off his towel his mouth on mine body against mine his hair his flesh, I was hard he was hard, I didn't fuck he wanted me to fuck him what else could I do. I grabbed his arse and pulled him closer if I was going to fuck him I was going to fuck him. I felt for his arsehole I pushed my finger into his arsehole, he winced he groaned he smiled a different smile, pushed himself into me I pushed him back down onto the mattress pushed his legs back, his arsehole up high, he grabbed his legs pulled them back, I leant down I licked his arsehole, I stuck my finger back in his arsehole, I stuck my tongue in next to my finger in his arsehole, his hand came round and he held the back of my head, he pushed my head into his arse who was in control. I fingered it, I put in another finger, I pulled his arsehole open I clamped my mouth over it I sucked on it I drew out his arsehole, another finger and another I mean really it was nearly my whole hand. I held nearly my whole hand in his arsehole, he looked in my eyes then looked down and away somewhere else looking away but looking inside, I came up and swallowed his cock all the way down, choked me, I kept the gob in my mouth I came up level with him, most of my hand still in his arsehole, I stayed above him I looked in his eye he was smiling I raised an eyebrow he got it he opened his mouth I gobbed in his open mouth, gob and its trail, he swallowed I kissed him what was it, 4.37am.

Fuck me, he said in my ear, fuck me. And so I wiggled my hand in his arse, oh fuck, he said, and then I pulled out my hand, looked down at his arsehole it was gaping wincing gaping. He'd put the condoms on the side I took one I opened it I put it on my cock, he was looking at me I was looking at him. I got some lube I lubed the condom I lubed his arsehole, the one my whole hand had nearly been in, I spat on it too but that was more for effect, I fingered it, one finger, two, three, four again, nearly my whole hand, fucked it with nearly my whole hand, and then I looked at him and said do you want it and he looked at me and he nodded and he said yeah and he looked at me like it was all he ever wanted and all he ever will want and maybe then it was. And so I put the head of my cock against his hole and I pushed in the tip and he said oh fuck and I pushed in some more he flinched ah fuck, he said, it was always this way, same for me, it takes a minute to accommodate it takes a minute to acclimatize it takes a minute to deal. He breathed out hard then short bursts and then his eyes widened he was ready if he knew it or not so I pushed and he screamed and grabbed my arse and held me for a millisecond and then he pulled on my arse he was pushing me in I pushed and I was all the way in, he grabbed me hard, I was kissing him, I held off moving, stayed deepest in him, and then I started to fuck, slowly to begin, he was whining, oh fuck he was saying, I was fucking quicker and quicker, pulled back so I was upright and slowed right down, so I could see my cock go in his hole, how his hole was responding to my cock, clenching on it, releasing, I took his legs in my hands, held them up, moved them, changed the angle of his hole, all I wanted was to get in deeper, then I grabbed his arse pulled it towards me sped up to shock him pounded it hard hard hard then pulled out he shouted, his hole was in shock, wide, I watched it clench, widen, clench, I watched it I watched it, and when it had clenched I pushed my cock in again all the way down to the hilt, came down on top of him again and hitched myself up to angle down into him, to push in harder deeper, I pulled up straight again, he was hard, had been the whole time, I took his balls in one hand, his cock in the other, started to jerk him, he closed his eyes, played with his nipples, was arching his back, I was jerking him and jerking him and he was moaning and moaning and then he looked at me he stared at me and said I'm close I'm close, and so I fucked harder and jerked and jerked and his back arched and arched and he moaned and said oh fuck fuck and he came, came hard cum over his head, second spurt on his face, third his chest, his hole clenched hard on my cock, clench release clench release, and that was it I came I came I fell on him I kissed him I pounded him I came I came into rubber all safe all sealed, what is from me can't be in him it can't. That morning I fucked three others then another guy fucked the life out of me. I got home at 6.47am. I opened the door I tried to be quiet I didn't want to wake Jerry but Jerry was already up, he was painting, a small rectangle scrap of wood, orange, blue, a circle, a line.

 Busy night dear, said Jerry. I looked at Jerry I said nothing I could say nothing.

 Good, said Jerry, I'm glad.

10

I'm looking for the line, Jerry would say, or, Where is the line, or, It's the line, or sometimes just, The line.

Maybe he said it to me that morning when I got back from the Coliseum, maybe he said it to me another time, maybe he said it to himself, maybe he said nothing.

It was our conversation then our loops our circularity, over months, Jerry home most of the time, those two years after he came out of hospital, those two years I worked at the Albion and I fucked and I partied and I loved Jerry and I loved our life I loved all we said to each other all that he said.

Jerry set up his easel by the glass doors, looking over his garden, but I never saw him paint his garden, at least not what his garden looks like to me. He said it was for the light. The morning light is my light, he said to me once, but also not saying to me, just saying it into the room, my ears my brain my body just happened to be there to receive it.

The strong morning light gave him background, striking just through the door window, hard onto the wall, specific, like a spot placed to do its work. The morning light through the glass doors was diffuse, a well, deep drawn. I love the morning as much as the night, said Jerry, and it was true that, our first few months, what happened in the morning was as important as what happened in the night, if more chaotic, more random, now more forgotten, because by morning our minds and our bodies were usually gone and remembering was not the purpose. But there was purpose in those mornings, to break from the regular, the prescribed, Jerry hadn't been out for a couple of years, not like our first months, never again after he was hospitalized, life had changed, his energy was gone, he could not have done it, he didn't want to mess with his meds, whatever little use they were doing, some actually harming him, what did we know. He did not go out, I went out, he loved mornings, the break from the regular, the prescribed, at dawn he painted.

Jerry was rude and Jerry was stubborn and Jerry was selfish. If he was painting he pretended to tolerate me but really he wanted me gone. Most of the time it was OK, most of the time I was still asleep, or I was still out, I was round some other guy's, or I was recovering from a shift at the Albion, upstairs in bed, at some other guy's, whichever, back then these things were still a novelty to me. I was gone, the space for Jerry was clear, that was what mattered, Alone together, he once said, and I knew what he meant, this was our companionship, the understanding of our togetherness, the knowledge of it, the nourishment, and our ability to be alone.

Painting for him was alone together. If I were to break his aloneness, he would snap, he would be brittle, or he would respond with some shadowplay thought from the deep, some response to a response to a response to an internal conversation that could never be transcribed, never be logged, his answer dredged in the disdain of his thousand voices deep, often just one word from Jerry that held all his thousand voices of disdain had to say, that one word from

Jerry, not turning, still facing his easel, one word to whatever it was I'd had to say:

Quite.

Or I could be asking something simple, me a dumb kid just coming downstairs saying stuff, something to express my interest, my solidarity, something basic, like, how's it going, to which he would say, can't you see, said with no inflection to make it a question, that is what he was saying, no question, can't you see.

I kept out of his way, as much as I could. When Jerry was painting those mornings, those mornings of those months, those last months, I was most aware this was his flat, this was his space, he delineated it, he set the rules, we were equals but the force of Jerry ruled, these were the parameters of the home, this is what happened here, it is what happens here, it is still what happens here, I still live like I am ruled by Jerry, it is how I still function, it is in the ritual and the wildness, how both could be the same, the wildness at the easel, the wildness in whatever he had done, I had done, to break the regular, the prescribed, at some point in the morning he would stop to take a break, if I were upstairs I would hear him, I would feel the energy change downstairs, from wildness to ritual, the intensity dissipated, it is real it is true, he created energy when he was making I could feel it, and when it was gone it was gone. He could make it again, no matter.

It was usually around ten thirty, eleven he would take a break, he would break from the wildness of his thinking for his rituals. By then I was usually awake or I would awaken for his rituals they became part of me they are still part of me. He would go to the sink and he would wash up whatever there was to wash up, we always washed up the next day we never washed up at night, plates stacked in the sink, a pile, it didn't matter, we'll do it when we do it, he'd say, I always wanted to be a house boy, he'd say, a houseproud slut.

I would hear him turn on the tap and move the plates around, working out how to begin. I would get up and I would go downstairs and I would help him. He would wash up and I would dry.

What am I to do with this anger, he said to me one morning, showing no anger, washing the cups of no outward value but that he cherished for their shape, how much they could hold, how they felt in the hand, larger rounded mugs for tea, straight-edged cups for coffee, always of a generous size, why have less, Jerry would say. I still drink from most of them, most have survived.

That is what he said, what am I to do with my anger, again not a question, a statement. He was washing a plate, he rinsed the plate, he passed the plate to me, I still have the plate, what anger, I said, the anger at my dying, he said, the anger at this travesty of living.

I must have reacted with a flinch, or said something like, are we a travesty, something like that, I can't remember.

Not us, not this, you know what I mean, he said, he was onto a bowl, a specific shape, a specific depth, he preferred it to a plate, it holds everything, he would say, I still have the bowl, I eat from it.

The functioning of life when life cannot function, he said, all I want is to function.

He passed me the bowl, I started to dry it, he began to wash another, the same. The night before he had made a bean stew.

This is it I am going you know that, he said. I am going, I am gone, it is the same. I can't function I don't function I won't function again.

I said something like, don't give up, or, there's so much else, I don't remember, kids' stuff, I was a kid.

There is nothing else, you know this. There is nothing else other than functioning. Love is function, desire is function, pleasure is function. If I cannot function I cannot love I cannot desire I cannot feel pleasure. To live is to function. I have never been allowed to live, I mean truly, I have lived in shadows, I have never lived, I have never functioned, I mean truly functioned.

He paused. And then, what a waste.

He was washing a saucepan, old and battered already then, I hated it, food always stuck to its bottom, burned easily, Jerry loved the pan, was sentimental about it, I never understood why, not long after he died I threw it out, no nostalgia.

We can make our little world all we want we can function within it we can flourish within it I love how we function you make me flourish I love you, said Jerry, something burnt stuck to the bottom of the pan, bits of stew, it would have annoyed me, it did not annoy Jerry, or if it did he hid it, didn't want to give me the satisfaction, he loved his pot, for whatever reason.

We can function in our little world but outside we acquiesce we have always acquiesced we have always given in we were brought up that way we were educated that way we can protest we can fight we can think we are making change but in the end we acquiesce.

These conversations hurt. I loved them I miss them. These

conversations happened often they were regular they were often over the same ground, a cat tamping, over and over, the same the same, it was necessary it was needed Jerry needed it I needed it. It was hard it was raw it was uncomfortable. I was so young often I didn't know what Jerry meant now I know what Jerry meant. He was in conversation with me then. He is in conversation with me now.

What do I do with this anger, he would say again, the same conversation, or the start of another conversation, another day, the end of another conversation, another day, there was no answer because he meant no question. The anger was there and that was it there was no appeasement.

What have I done to you what have you become you don't deserve this these aren't your burdens you should be free, he would say, like he had to say it, he had to say the words, though he knew my responses, or versions of them, I was the happiest I'd ever been, he had saved me, I was free, he was no burden, he had unlocked everything.

What am I to do with this anger, he would say, and it was like he had always been saying it, long before me, all his life, saying it to push himself somewhere else, the anger he'd always had and always would have, the anger compounded, the anger growing as he was dying, for he was dying, it was happening in front of me, he was going, there had been a change, vitality had been there and now vitality was not there and that was it. But there was still anger and the anger grew. He did not aim the anger at me I was no punching bag I would never have let him that was not how things were. He was with his anger and he faced his anger and he wanted to understand his anger. Ritual helped him be with his anger don't you see anger is function just as is love. This ritual this morning ritual so boring we washed up we dried up so boring it was everything. When we were done with the dishes we made coffee and something to eat, porridge or toast or boiled eggs, Jerry able to eat less and less, Jerry knew he was deteriorating, Jerry couldn't stop the deterioration.

What will you do Johnny, said Jerry one time, again not a question, I had no answer, he needed no answer, do you see? This was our in-between state, beyond questions, where you go when you face anger, be with anger, instead of giving in, be with love, I did not know what I would do and it did not matter. When I was angry Jerry helped me be with that anger, I am angry and Jerry helps me be with that anger.

I'll get by, I'd say, you know I'll get by, and he'd say, I know you'll get by you little fucker.

Terms of endearment.

What am I to do with this anger, he would say, I would have finished eating, he would have eaten what he could, not much, the plates in the sink, the cups too, straight sided specific for coffee, his eyes were back on the scrap of wood on his easel, he might have been talking but his eyes were elsewhere, his mind, he was looking at what he had done he was thinking of what he would do, what else could he do, where was the line.

What he could do with his anger was that he could paint and he could paint and he could try to find the line. He could try to find the line knowing he would never find the line, it didn't matter, knowing he would not know what to do with his anger, it didn't matter, that frail thing, tiny before, now all bone.

11

There are 127 paintings left now, that I know of anyway, most with me, or Gareth, Fiona, other friends. There were many more, Jerry would destroy them, he didn't care, I found him snapping work once, a scrap of wood he had painted, red rectangle, blue circle, yellow behind it, I thought it was beautiful, I told him so, this made him snap it even harder, why the fuck would I want to be part of this society's idea of legacy, he said, his words like all his words: deliberate, measured.

   That day he called the purge, snapped or broke painting after painting, he let me save two, one diagonals of red, yellow, the other just variations of blue, they're yours to deal with, he said, not my problem, he broke the wood, snapped, different thicknesses, different sizes, the purge had a purpose, he used the wood to make a herb bed, compact, just for what we needed, sage, rosemary, thyme, oregano, a separate small bed for mint, a bully, will take over everything. I offered him help Jerry wanted no help he had nails he had a hammer he made sure with each piece the painted side was turned inwards, none of his work was visible, no marks no colour no line, all turned inwards to face and hold the soil, the edge for the roots as they eventually grew out and realized their limit. Just around the inside top his colour and his line could sometimes be seen, when the soil compressed, or after heavy rain, I don't want to see it, Jerry would say, mulch it, and so he would mulch it, we would cover what could be seen of his colour, his line, what is it anyway, he would say, it's just wood, don't pretend otherwise.

He loved his herb bed it survived him by fourteen years, by then the wood had rotted through at the front, there was no real pretence of form any more, the soil spilling out of it, the mint long since taken over, the bully, I took what was left of the wood apart, flakes of Jerry's colour, his line, peeling off among the scraps but really nothing, but then at the back a section that was firmer, maybe it had been out of the rain, the soil had found its own drainage against the back fence the wood was still stiff, I dug out all the soil I took it all apart, and there, snapped, was the red rectangle, the blue circle, the yellow behind, in two parts, tatty but still what it was, what was I to do, I am not Jerry, Jerry was gone, what would Jerry do Jerry would put it on the compost Jerry would see it decompose, I am not Jerry I cannot pretend to be Jerry I am not him, I dried the wood and I brushed off the soil and then I did what I knew Jerry would have hated, an act of violence, he would have called it, sacrilege. I glued the two bits together. Before I knew of 126 of Jerry's paintings and now there were 127.

Jerry could live with some of his paintings they weren't all destroyed many survived, he was proud of many of them he wanted to look at many of them it was like he continued to work on them even if they were finished even if he never touched them again. One was of areas of yellow picked out by black line against red. Another was areas of blue picked out in pink line against green. Others like them were destroyed, were painted over, these two stayed, Jerry put them on the wall, they do not match, one is on a single piece of wood, square, maybe an old cupboard door, the other painting is on slats of wood nailed together, heads of the nails visible under the paint, the paint over the heads with its own smoothness, one happened, then the other, I don't remember when Jerry painted them, Jerry never wrote on them a date, never named them, never signed them, they are not me, he would say, I do not make them they just happen. He would say this, or words like this, over and again, I would look amused and Jerry knew I was amused and Jerry liked that I was amused, Jerry knew I wouldn't mock him Jerry knew I wouldn't question him, what he was doing was not up for questioning, Jerry was doing what Jerry was doing, he only put certain works on the wall, certain ones put in certain places and Jerry would stare at them and stare at them and stare at them and it was continual it was endless it was like he was finding endlessness when he knew there was end.

Maybe there are others in the world, who knows, Jerry would have said he did not care legacy is a lie and maybe he was right. I do not make them, he would say, when all he would do was make them. I did not understand but then I did not need to understand it was not about understanding I learned that from Jerry. What was happening felt right and it felt real and this was what mattered I learned everything from him. I was young and he taught me how to be.

He would not ask me about his work he was not seeking praise he needed no validation. Someone asked him once, how much are they worth, and Jerry just said, ten thousand pounds, and then he said, each, and whoever it was looked startled and said, who would pay that, and Jerry just shrugged he had no idea the thought of money the thought of value was ludicrous to him he just said that amount that was it. No one ever bought one no one ever paid that amount, Jerry never thought anyone would, that was not his interest that was not his purpose. I have kept them I will keep them I will look after them what will happen to them when I die I do not know.

Why am I doing this why bother no one cares he said once, the self-pity that needs its release, the self-pity that can build up and build up and take over if it is not checked, better that it be released, let out the self-pity let it go let it be. It was summer it was solstice, a day or two before or maybe after, air pressure was high there was no moisture no clouds just light just heat, the garden door open from before dawn, open as soon as Jerry woke, Jerry had begun sleeping downstairs, on the daybed, he said it was to be closer to the easel, so he could look at his work in the night, so he would not wake me first thing, but I knew it was a cover, he knew it was a cover, he could no longer face the stairs, they made him dizzy they made him out of breath.

Is she still alive dear, it was Gareth, how grim is her reaper.

He came for tea, I made the tea. Gareth helped Jerry outside, the sun was strong, I may as well be a corpse with a tan, said Jerry.

They sat.

Your tomatoes are growing strong, said Gareth. Going to be a good crop this year.

I won't be here to eat them, said Jerry. It was hard for him to talk, fungus growing in his throat, he was being taken over, pushed out. I am, said Jerry, literally rotting.

His sentences came broken, pauses for pain, physical pain, mental pain.

I'm going to miss you, said Gareth.

Maybe you'll breathe me in someday, said Jerry.

How old are you, said Gareth.

Five thousand and one, said Jerry. How about you.

Born the same year, said Gareth.

You will live, said Jerry, to the age of five thousand and forty-two. At least.

Lucky world, said Gareth.

I poured the tea. There were biscuits, I'd made them the day before, shortbread.

What were we doing, said Jerry, when we were young. When we were alive.

I was minding my own business, said Gareth, a normal little boy from the suburbs. Then you came along, this whirlwind, just back from Europe.

Europe, said Jerry.

I was all eyes, said Gareth, I couldn't believe you existed, you were so beautiful.

Were, said Jerry. How rude, said Jerry. You little bitch, said Jerry.

You know what I mean, said Gareth. What was that, twenty years ago. Only twenty years ago. We were nothing.

Still are, said Jerry. He coughed, he sipped his tea, Gareth did the same, no one spoke for a while, no one needed to, we were in sun. Jerry's eyes were closed, Jerry's mouth was closed then Jerry's mouth opened Jerry's lips pulled back

Jerry's teeth showed themselves Jerry's teeth were apart a gap between his teeth. Skin tight over his cheekbones flesh gone just skin just bone his mouth open his teeth, air trying to enter, this is how he will be, I remember thinking, I remember it, this is how he will be, this is dying.

A car went by, a bird threatened another, someone screamed in the street, I don't remember, something jolted us to life, Jerry alerted again, Jerry reacclimatizing, back in this world, his eyes caught mine, I was still staring at him, he smiled and his mouth was still open and his teeth still showed and there was a gap between, air trying to get in, he smiled and his eyes said all they needed to say, his eyes said, I know.

Gareth and Jerry both sipped their tea, the air was to be filled, it needed filling, but still for a while it could not be filled, what did Gareth want to say, it was for Gareth to say.

Remember I tried to make you my boyfriend, said Gareth.

You were so sweet, said Jerry.

That's what you said to me then, said Gareth.

What was that.

You're so sweet.

Did I.

You did. Twenty-two years and eight months and I don't know how many days ago.

Well you are.

What.

You are so sweet.

And that was not enough for you.

Jerry smiled Jerry was still smiling, Jerry smiled.

I didn't want anything, said Jerry, don't you see.

Jerry paused and Jerry coughed.

I didn't want anything then, I don't want anything now. When you say that you were not enough for me, it is meaningless, not enough, too much, it's all the same thing, I didn't want a boyfriend then, I don't want a boyfriend now, no offence to you Johnny, I love you, you are everything to me. But it is different. There is no possession. I don't want anything. I never have. I never will.

I could take it I wanted to hear it I wanted to know. Gareth was looking at me maybe Gareth was seeing if I could take it maybe he was jealous that was it he was jealous. Jealous of what, what he didn't understand. What was I, a kid, I understood, or at least I felt, I felt first and then from what I felt I understood. The feeling always came first, they always come first now, words later, those words might then sound harsh, it's OK, the words were standing for what I felt, it's OK, Jerry taught me that.

I didn't want anything, Jerry said, I never have ever. I escaped that world, ownership, the world of my parents. He paused, he coughed, he paused. That loveless world.

Jerry was talking straight ahead, eyes closed again, face tilted up to the sun.

He coughed, he tried to keep talking, pain on his face of pain. And so when we met, my dear Gareth, Jerry said, I was in my militant stage of refusal, I didn't want anything, and it just so happens that not wanting anything was to last the rest of my life, right up here, to the end.

What has that refusal brought you Jerry.

Love.

They were both silent for a moment, Jerry head tilted back, eyes closed, mouth open, smiling. Gareth was sitting eyes open, looking out to the garden, he sat and he sat and I realized he was crying, quietly. He was crying, he could contain it, the tears could fall in silence, they fell, he felt what he felt, in silence.

I was well practised, Gareth said to me the other week, I'd gone round to see him my regular visit, he'd asked me to get him dried goods, dried beans, dried chickpeas, rice, flour. When Jerry died I'd already spent what twelve thirteen years crying at bedsides. You get used to it, the silent cry.

Gareth was crying and looking out to the garden and he felt me gaze and so he turned his eyes to me and he shook his head and Gareth was crying. I did not cry I did not cry I did not cry. Gareth wiped his eyes Gareth stopped crying. Jerry had his eyes closed Jerry had not moved. Jerry said, maybe some wine is called for, don't you think, or some vodka.

Gareth laughed, I laughed, Jerry opened his eyes.

I got vodka first, the bottle in the freezer. Jerry liked it neat, we drank it neat.

Gareth that awful house you were living in, those awful people you called friends, you wouldn't leave, it took months, you were so scared, why were you so scared.

Jerry you and the warehouse were against all that I had been taught how to be, and you were all that I wanted.

We got you in the end.

That first warehouse was awful, that first winter. Unbearable. How did we survive.

It was glorious.

No walls, no separation of our lives.

So much fun.

We have always had different ideas of fun.

Jerry could not move his head but he raised his eyebrows.

When we were kicked out I was so scared I was so happy. You loved the sheds.

I love the sheds.

What were the sheds, I asked.

Jerry opened his eyes. He was smiling. The third warehouse I lived in, the second for Gareth. There were eleven of us by then, four or five were couples, it changed.

It changed often, said Gareth.

What were the sheds, I asked again.

I told you about Michael, said Jerry. He built us sheds. That was all there was. A warehouse floor, six sheds, for sleeping in.

They were spaced out, Gareth said, so you could make noise and others wouldn't hear you.

Fucking, said Jerry.

Others wouldn't hear you fucking, said Gareth. Wouldn't hear you so much.

Everyone was fucking all the time.

Remember when Dennis came for the summer.

I remember when Dennis came for the summer.

Who was Dennis, I asked.

Dennis was from New York. He fucked. That's what he did. He fucked me. Several times.

He did not fuck me, said Gareth. Did he fuck everyone else.

I think he fucked everyone else.

He was so funny, said Gareth, so beautiful, so kind. He was such a gentleman. He told me his story. Do you remember Jerry? Dennis said to me, and I will try to do his accent, forgive me, 'Daddy came back from the war and he got my momma pregnant and I was the result and so continued his disappointment in the world. What can I do but continue to disappoint him.' He'd have been what, twenty-three.

Where is Dennis now, I asked.

He died.

They were both silent for a while, Jerry was looking down. He sipped his vodka. He closed his eyes again. Gareth was looking at him, I was looking at him.

This light now was the light then, Jerry managed to say, it is the same. He coughed, he paused. We lived in the light, the sunlight, the moonlight. That was what guided us. Don't you see. The city around us disappeared, we were in our own world.

Jerry stopped Jerry paused Jerry wanted to continue he needed to continue.

There were the sheds and then, Jerry was speaking slowly and specifically, by the windows, above the river, there were sofas and daybeds and floor cushions and mattresses and chairs and blankets and rugs. There was a record player. There was a film projector. There were books. It was all we needed. Michael had met an architect in America who was thinking about the lives us queers lived, how our queerness was spatial, that we didn't want to live in a fucking home made for straight people. We needed a different way of being. We need a different way of being. It was a different use of a space, different priorities, what mattered was sharing, community. It's what we try and do in this space now, my dear Johnny.

You said this will not last, said Gareth. I remember. We were up on the roof.

It was as clear to me as the money coursing by us, that

river of wealth, it had ebbed out, we could live in the wreckage, but it would return, as sure as the tide.

I couldn't see it, said Gareth. I thought it was our wasteland playground for ever.

I wish I could have lived with your positive outlook.

You were always so very polite when calling me stupid.

Gareth had his hand on Jerry's arm, they were laughing. And then they were silent.

I used to think how we lived was so pioneering, such radicals, but now I realize that we were doing what humans have done for millennia, living communally, in groups. It is only in this very recent history that we have become so segregated and so removed from one another, and this forces those of us who believe in communality to be seen as militant.

Jerry was talking slowly, each word considered.

You radicalized me, said Gareth.

You must keep going, said Jerry. For me.

I will, Jerry, I will.

What we had then is not broken. It is still here. It will always be here.

It's so hard, said Gareth. You made it this far. You're not supposed to die.

You have to keep going, said Jerry, and now he was looking at me. You have to keep going.

He held my eye and he held my eye and then he smiled.

Maybe a touch more vodka, he said.

I got the bottle from the freezer, I poured some more.

You have been a good friend to me Gareth.

I am a good friend to you Jerry.

Let me say it. You have been a good friend to me. I value

your friendship and I appreciate it. I always have done. You have taught me much about friendship. You have shown me that at its heart it is not transaction, it is care. I am so grateful to you for showing me that. I have always been very good at seeming like I know what I'm doing, and of course I do not. Before I met you I was so sure of myself, that is how I presented, free in the world, but I had not known true friendship, I had lived on camaraderie, that had been my fuel through life, that had lit me like a firecracker, the camaraderie of men, the transience, the immediacy of connection, I revelled in it, and I thought I knew it all and then I met you. Gareth you have shown me constancy and care. I am a nightmare I know I am. I am a little shit. I get away with anything I have been horrible I am vile I am difficult.

No, said Gareth.

I am not fishing, Jerry started coughing Jerry coughed. I am trying to speak plainly. It is hard. Let me speak. It was very hard for all of us at the end, when they torched the warehouse. It was clear we could not continue as we were. Or at least we could not continue as we were in this city, with how it was changing, or how it was revealing itself. We had to disperse and we had to go underground, in a way, to survive. And this was before people started dying. It is easy to think that the two are linked but they are not linked.

Jerry was gasping for air like he would not stop until he had said all he had to say. He coughed, he sipped his vodka, he continued, slowly.

We were already down and then we were kicked even harder. A life of being kicked. When we were young and we had our own world, friendship was easy. When we had to leave that world, when we had to enter this world, I know I was difficult, I was stubborn. I changed, or rather, I revealed more of who I was. Maybe it was that others from the warehouses had begun to conform. Maybe it was because our friends started to die. But I began to feel very different, sometimes very isolated, I don't know if I've ever told you that.

We've talked about it, said Gareth, allowing for Jerry's need to go over it again, this was often the reality of conversation, going over and over, until something is understood or at least can be lived with or that something else comes along that buries it.

I felt very isolated but you were always there, I knew you were always there, and we may not have seen each other for months, sometimes, but I knew you were there.

You are using the past tense again, said Gareth.

I am in the past tense, said Jerry. He looked down he looked at Gareth and tried to smile. He looked at me, and tried to smile.

Maybe some wine, some cheese and some bread would help.

I was OK being servant. I went inside, sliced some bread thin, cut it into quarters, there was cheddar in the fridge, brie. I put it on a tray, some olive oil, some salt. Three tumblers, a bottle of wine, white. I carried the tray back out to my love and his friend.

Thank you, Jerry said to me, my darling. I loved it when Jerry called me his darling, I can hear him saying it to me now, I poured out three tumblers of wine, took the bottle back inside, into the fridge, back outside Gareth was saying, the idea that you have of yourself is so counter to the way I see you, and the way that I think most people see you. Jerry you are the most gregarious, the most welcoming, the most companionable human I have ever met and will now probably ever meet. I love when you are stubborn, I love when you are a little shit, you give me life, you have given me so much life.

Jerry was crying. Gareth put his arm around Jerry and he held him.

I want you both to go ahead. And go on. You have to.

Jerry was speaking, his head down, Gareth his arm around him, Jerry's voice quiet and soft. Jerry looked up, looked me in the eye.

What else are you going to do, he said, and it was a command and a threat as much as a question.

Jerry drank from his wine. Gareth my dear, how many times have we said that we never want to go through this again, and now we are going through this again, and now it is me who is dying.

I'm so scared, said Gareth.

We know it, said Jerry. We've seen it. We face it.

Jerry sipped some more wine.

Look at this garden. How beautiful it is. How lucky am I to have had a garden. It has grown. How lucky am I to have been born into this nightmare. This broken world, it does not give a damn about me I don't need it to. Does it give a damn about anyone or anything that's not the point. We can just do what we do everyday, to listen, to care, to be humble, to make. I am slightly tipsy I am grateful for it I would like to be drunk.

I have all the time for you my friend, said Gareth.

My cosmic friend, said Jerry. I wish we had a roof to climb up now, to be in this solstice. But we have this garden.

Jerry smiled at me, that cosmic smile. I was a spectator, conversation doesn't have to mean involvement, conversation can mean presence. Gareth and Jerry needed me there, they wouldn't be able to say what they were saying to each other without an audience, I was that audience.

Gareth will you take some of my paintings home with you. I have made too many of them they are worthless I'll throw them away if you don't.

I would love to have more of your paintings Jerry.

You don't have to I don't know why anyone would want them I'll throw them away, said Jerry, which translated as, I am so happy you want them I am so embarrassed I can't deal with my embarrassment I am embarrassed that I'm embarrassed I'm just a kid underneath it all just a child tell me it's going to be OK tell me.

Please Jerry, said Gareth. It would be my honour to live with them. If it makes you feel any better about yourself I can pay you for them.

Fuck off, said Jerry, he was thrilled. I may need to use the bathroom, what do you think, could you help me up.

Jerry was trying to stand on his own, I was there, I gave him my hands, I pulled him up, my muscleman, he said to me, I said, your mind is definitely gone if you think I'm a muscleman, or something like that, the words lost in holding him, words said in breathing to help him up, my sweet sad incapable tipsy thing, the light so brilliant outside, deep dark inside, perspective playing its strange tricks, how far it was to go just a few steps, our curtain framing, hanging heavy to the side, pushed against the wall but performing its role, what we see, how we see it, how we live, how we see where we live, Jerry pointed to it as we went by, remember this Gareth, he said, turning round, turning his whole body round, incapable of just turning his head, it was his drunkenness, how he was in drunkenness, but it was how he was going to be soon always, unsteady and unsure, incapable,

We might need to speed up dear, Jerry said, and so we bustled through to get there I got his trousers down I sat him down on the toilet I got him there,

Thank you my dear, Jerry said to me.

I love you, I said to Jerry.

I am so lucky, said Jerry.

When he was done I got him outside again, are you OK out here, I said to him on the way, more more more, said Jerry, always more.

I sat him down, could you get me my cardigan, he said, and more wine,

He has you where he wants you, said Gareth.

I have me where I want me, I said to Gareth, I was happy to oblige, I would do anything for Jerry, I would do anything. I put on a record, Sylvester, 'I Who Have Nothing'. Sun almost down now, I took a sweater out for Gareth, in case he wanted it, I handed it to him and he made no movement, except an involuntary pulling back of the skin on his face, nostrils flared,

Picky bitch, said Jerry, under his breath over his breath, hate as love, and then Jerry said, let me look at you Gareth, stand up, let me see you.

Ha, Gareth said, supermodel. He stood and twirled like he had on a skirt or a dress that would twirl, that about him would have movement, except on his body was a white T-shirt, crewneck, a plaid shirt, its sleeves rolled up tight, to an exact length, blue denim jeans, belted. White socks, white tennis shoes.

Always a feast, said Jerry. The specifics! We should learn, Johnny, we are such schlubs. If only I had learned the specifics of life where would I be.

Jerry smiled, a smile to say he knew there were no specifics, this was it, this is it, that's all there is.

Gareth went in to piss.

How are you doing, I said to Jerry.

Terribly, said Jerry. Couldn't be happier. That scent.

It was the tobacco plant. Jerry loved it, I grow it for Jerry now.

I could die in that scent, said Jerry, knowing what he was saying, and what he was saying broke me. I cried. I didn't know what else to do. Jerry took my hand, it's OK, he said, it's OK.

Gareth came out, saw us, stood in the doorway, was silent for a moment. I think I might telephone to order us some pizza.

Marvellous, said Jerry, he was clasping my hand, gripping it, energizing me.

I was done. Gareth took over. He got more wine, changed the record, Norma Lewis, 'Maybe This Time'. Doorbell rang, it was the pizza, Gareth answered it, Gareth paid, Gareth put the boxes on a picnic table, Gareth got us paper towels. The pizza was good the pizza was terrible, same thing. It was dark. Gareth and I ate, Jerry did not.

Let's play favourite fucks, said Jerry. You first.

He looked at Gareth.

Two lads I took home from the Albion dear, said Gareth. They were friends and they had never seen each other naked until I came along. I fucked them both all night, one after the other, or switching mid-fuck. I would be fucking one and fingering the other. Or eating their arse. I fucked them till dawn then we rested then I fucked them again.

Gareth have you ever been fucked.

Nope.

Our dear cosmic friend the bossy top, said Jerry. What about you Johnny, who was your favourite fuck.

He looked at me, I could see what he was doing, trying to bring life, I tried to bring life. I told them a story about a guy whose dick was as thick as a can of Coke.

Romance, said Jerry, is not dead, unlike me.

How about you Jerry.

He was like an apparition, said Jerry. He was talking so slowly it was like he was seeing an apparition. I was so young. It was in Italy, I had been away already for a few months, I thought I knew what I was doing but I didn't know what I was doing. I was in some bar, he came along, really he was nothing, a scrawny thing, not much older than me, he would not tell me his name, he was so familiar, why would I need to know his name, it was part of the game. He was intoxicating. We were talking in the bar, but it was like he had broken into my personal space, he inhabited me, and this is before we went back to the room where I was staying, he would not tell me where he lived, would not tell me his story, anything, but I felt like I knew him, maybe that is what it is like when you are being charmed, or seduced, it didn't matter, he activated me, it was so simple, he turned on a switch in me, we went back to my room and he was nothing like your Coke can, more like the top of a Coke bottle, but he knew what to do with it, oh man he knew what to do with me. I was for ever electrified. He made me see something of myself, of what I could do and who I could be, liberated from time, or at least the time in which we were living, in which we are living, he still has that effect on me. He fucked me and he held me and then he left, and as he left he said, I will see you in winter. He was earnest and I was charmed and I thought how sweet, how adorable, and I thought it was just talk. But then five months later it was winter and he appeared, it was the same, it was real, whatever else he was in his life, whatever else he couldn't tell me, with me it was real and that was all I needed and I never saw him again.

We stayed up to see the moon, then we stayed up some more, voices into the dark. Gareth was talking when I realized that Jerry had fallen asleep, head slumped forward, neck barely able to bear the weight of brain skull skin whatever flesh was left, like his head could just snap off and roll onto the ground.

I woke him gently. He was gone and gone. Gareth helped, we lifted him, him between us his arms over our shoulders, got him to the couch, the couch his friends had made, covered him with a sheet, it was all he needed, a glass of water by him. Gareth wanted to tidy outside I didn't want to tidy outside I helped Gareth tidy outside.

Take care of him, Gareth said when he left, and yourself.

I went up to bed, cried, fell asleep. Noise downstairs woke me. It was Jerry, getting up to paint while he still could, trying to find the line.

12

I wrote twenty-one letters to Jerry that July, one each day, before he died. I wrote the letters in the morning, before visiting time, posted them, most would arrive next day, sometimes a delay. I posted them on Sundays too, even though there was no post, I wrote what I wrote and then went to visit him and usually told him the stories I'd just written, him getting the letter with the same news the day later. I wrote even when he could no longer hold the letter, could no longer focus, could no longer speak, last letters of few words, mostly drawings: hearts, stars, flowers.

    I have all the letters, Jerry kept them, then the nurses kept them for Jerry. Some are unopened. I have the first one here. This is what I wrote.

To my love Jerry.
    I couldn't sleep without you here so I came and lay down on the sofa where you would be, and I watched the dawn over your garden, it reminds me of you.
    My Jerry be strong, you have come home from hospital before, you will come home again.
    I am drinking coffee from your mug, eating toast with the

marmalade you made. Your easel is here for you waiting. I will weed and water don't you worry.

You can keep going Jerry I know you can. I don't have to go into the Albion, Paul says I can miss as many shifts as I need, he will still pay me. He says he loves you and he needs you. I will see you in a couple of hours I can't wait to see you. I will get the tube and then walk. I will be there everyday Jerry every single day.

I love you
your
Johnny

I drew hearts around his name and my name, stars, flowers. We'd taken Jerry to hospital the night before. Jerry couldn't breathe he couldn't walk his temperature was scary he needed care. Gareth drove us, they admitted Jerry straight away, it just so happens, said the nurse, we have a private room for you.

They put Jerry on oxygen they put Jerry on a drip, Jerry seemed better for just being there, there was safety in the environment with all its peril. Goodnight, said Jerry before I left, sleep well, I love you. I left the room and closed the door and then I went back in again and kissed him on top of his head, held his head. I cried. Goodnight Jerry, I said.

Gareth had stayed with me Gareth drove me home. Gareth dropped me at home. I was home. Jerry was not home. I knew Jerry would not be coming home.

First day I went to see him I said, shall I bring you flowers from the garden, he said, don't you dare cut them.

Some of the nurses were the same as before, he's already ruling the roost, said one who remembered him.

The grande dame, said Jerry.

I was telling Jerry about some drama from the Albion, some irrelevancy, someone had said something about someone else, or something, it seemed important to me then, or maybe I was just trying to keep the lifeblood going, there was no pretence, not pretending everything was OK, I was not hiding from anything, maybe just talking was helping my brain whirr over, I don't know, I was saying it, holding Jerry's hand, oh really, he'd say, no, he'd say, tell me more.

A doctor came in, a junior with him, hello Jerry, said the doctor, hello, the doctor said to me, looking at me, this is Johnny, said Jerry, he is family.

Jerry I'm going to be straightforward with you. You have an infection and right now your body is struggling to fight it. Your T-cell count is in single figures. We are going to do all we can to help you Jerry. You are in the right place. Let's try and get your strength up and get your body to fight the infection. Do you have any questions.

Can you give Jerry any medication, I asked.

Jerry is already on antibiotics, to try to beat the infection, said the doctor. This is all the medication we have available. I know you understand, there is no point pussyfooting around.

Never pussyfoot, said Jerry.

OK I'll check in on you tomorrow, said the doctor, there was a sink, he washed his hands, his junior washed her hands, they left.

It's what we knew already, said Jerry, his hand still holding mine, gripping it, energizing it. Let us do what we can. That is all there is.

Jerry had a view with trees. From his bed he saw trees, not the car park below.

Jerry was bored. Jerry was restless. Jerry was scared. Jerry tried. Jerry could be vivacious. I took in pencils I took in paper. Jerry drew and he drew and he drew. The nurse would say, do you want me to turn on the TV, and Jerry would say, why would I want to end my life with indoctrination.

Gareth had a spare cassette player Jerry didn't have cassettes. I had my old cassettes, Gareth made cassettes, friends made cassettes, songs from their days in the warehouses, songs from the discos, tracks from the clubs, songs that Jerry had heard over and over and now he heard them again.

My frail little bird in that bed, he held court, friends and friends and friends came, a sea of friends, so many I had never met, oh I've heard all about you, they would say, or words like that, the one who finally settled him down, I would smile, not counter them, settled down, the total opposite of my life with Jerry, he ignited me, he gave me the world, I let them say it, settled down, it didn't matter, what mattered was they were here for Jerry, some I could tell he would rather not see, friendships that had seemed for ever in the moment then a moment later didn't exist, they came to visit and I could tell that Jerry would rather never see them again, the exquisite torture, him trapped in their presence, Jerry forced to play the role of the grateful.

And then there were those who made Jerry smile and smile and smile, you came, he would say, it's you, look at you, he would say, stand over there, let me see you. Stand at the end of the bed, he would say, directing the room, you, all I see all day is that wall, I want to look at you, let me drink you in.

If he heard someone was coming he would say, tell them

to wear something fabulous. Is Peter coming? Oh good, Jerry said. Peter arrived in a long leather coat, oh hello Peter, Jerry said, stand at the end of the bed, would you be a dear.

   Of course, said Peter, he stood at the end of the bed, his hands in the pockets of his long leather coat, he stood there for a while, staring at Jerry, Jerry stared back, Peter was smiling, Peter put his hands to his top button and unbuttoned it. He put his hands to his next button and unbuttoned it. And the next. And the next. His leather coat was open, and then Peter shrugged it off. It fell to the floor. Peter stood there in just a jockstrap. Peter smiled at Jerry.

   How marvellous, said Jerry.

   It's all for you, said Peter, always.

   Peter put on his show, the show we had all seen, in various forms, over and over, he put on his show, libidinous body in this place of bodies in peril, filth among the sterile, what is filth, the body doing what it wants, Jerry's body going, I remember the first time looking at him when he was more skull than flesh, that the flesh left on his body was no cushion to hide the skull, his bone beneath the eye socket his bone where there should have been cheek, now skin stretched over bone, skin unable to hide the bone beneath, I remember when I first saw it, we were alone, the two of us in his room, Jerry was looking out the window, he was lost, focused in his lostness, I was present, to be witness to his lostness, we had no need for words, Jerry in his bed lost staring out the window, me sitting at his side, sitting facing his side, it was then I first saw it, his sunkenness, his death, it was here, death present before death, death present for days, weeks, his death in the room with us, his death making its demands of his body, his death in charge now, it held sway, entering him through pain, sat up in bed knees up what was left of his body full clench, as if Jerry was trying to push something out of him, to push out death, but death had taken its hold. Jerry grabbed my hand he gripped me he gripped me he released, a pause, summoning his powers, whatever powers he had left, trying to push out the death that was him and he was death.

I wrote my letters to Jerry every day, every day I posted them to Jerry, the nurses on the ward would hold onto my letters for when I had gone, for when visiting time was over, to give to Jerry late at night, or early in the morning, with each letter I sent images cut from magazines, postcards, photos, snapshots of us together, naked on a beach, where we weren't meant to be naked but we were naked, gardening in swimming trunks, as naked as we could be in our garden of Nova Scotia House, our swimming trunks tiny, really we may as well have been naked, it had been a day spent tending to our garden then cooking with what had been grown, really it was more assembling in that heat, lettuce, radishes, little onions, the first few tomatoes, with flatbreads, cheese, pot of lentils, wine, wine and wine, our days had been delicious, but now death was here, I wanted Jerry to remember the deliciousness, I remember arriving as soon as visiting hours began, the day he should have got that photo, of us in the garden, Jerry was distracted, Jerry was bothered, looking for something, this little sparrow lost in his nest, There you are dear, Jerry said, I remember his words still his words but the sores of his mouth muffling them, taking him out of his words, death taking over, I can't find my pencil where is my pencil can you see it.

In this world, in Jerry's world, this was what mattered, his pencil, its location, his need to find it, his need for everything to be OK, it would not be OK, for Jerry, ever again. I said I would help him, I tried to find his pencil, I could not find his pencil, I need to write my list, said Jerry. I tried to calm Jerry, Jerry would not be calmed, there was no solace. I said to Jerry, I can get you another pencil, Jerry brushed his hand in front of his face, like he was brushing away what I had just said, like he didn't want a solution. He wanted to stay fixed in his own narrative, I don't know, he said, not to me, saying it to himself, death taking over, the internalization.

I came from the moon and now I'm just dirt ready to renew, said Jerry, another day, he had been given morphine, morphine was talking.

We were alone, it was a Wednesday afternoon. Jerry was speaking and I was listening.

It is a continual, don't you see Johnny, it is continual. Atoms dirt everything. I am nothing. It seems broken but it is continual.

What is broken, I asked him.

Our queer magic, said Jerry. It is real and beyond time and beyond sickness and beyond those fucking bastards, the politicians, the legislators, the moralizers, so-called leaders, my contemporaries who are my enemies. Queer magic is alive queer magic will always be alive. How many of us have died how many of us will have to die.

Jerry tried to reach for water he could not reach for water. I helped him reach for water. There was a straw I held it to his lips he tried to suck he could not suck, could not take any water, his sores, his exhaustion, his end.

The line it is there it is not broken I can see it.

Jerry was looking off out beyond at nothing at everything.

I have fallen from the line I am over I am gone it does not matter the line exists.

What is the line, I asked Jerry.

Continuity, acceptance, bravery, vulnerability, patience, anger, insight, pleasure, care, beauty, stubbornness. It is love it is love it is love.

Jerry looked at me as he said this and he smiled, morphine smile.

What was I meant to be other than myself. That is all. To be myself and not what was expected of me, of that poor little fucker who was named Jerry Field, expected to marry, to father children in a marriage, to work for someone so to make that someone profit, little of which I would see, to conform, by doing so to convince others too to conform, to become part of the conforming mass, each time someone conforms, every single time, they do damage, it may seem irrelevant, it may seem nothing, but to conform is to eradicate, poor little Jerry Field, how I weep for him and what he will face.

Jerry was quiet for a while, a quiet I knew was thought, a quiet which usually led to a continuation of thought, an argument taken from somewhere else, a fresh take, a correction of something he had just said, a clarification, an offshoot of thought that became his main thought, for a while, Jerry had always been in control, in control of thought that was free flowing, but now thoughts fell from his brain, connection gone, precision and insight then confusion, doubt, as if the thought from seconds ago was a thought from decades past, thought from long before I knew him, he was within this vastness, the expanse beyond age, frightened wise desperate sad, Jerry was setting sail into the vastness, he had always been on its shores, always aware of the vastness, or maybe that's just how it appeared to me, I was so young, I knew nothing, what did I know, I was so scared, so frightened, I went every day, every hour I could, I was there, it is what you do it is what I did.

I was holding Jerry's hand, Jerry's hand straight upwards, Jerry's hand now mostly bone dressed with failed skin,

The cruelty, said Jerry, it is so cruel, I won't be there to look after you, I'm so sorry Johnny, I have let you down.

Jerry was sobbing Jerry was speaking the two were the same.

I've let you down, I don't know what to do Johnny I don't know what to do.

I did not know what to do, I knew words were useless, why lie, why pretend, I did not know what to do I could not tell him otherwise and so I held his hand and held his hand and held his hand.

What am I going to do Johnny, he paused and he wailed a silent wail like there couldn't be words just wail, the action of wail, no noise, his mouth as wide as can be to emit everything but no noise came, then the wail turned again to words, what am I going to do.

I tried to comfort him when there was no comfort. I stroked his arm. I put my head to his head. It hurt him to be held. I could not hold him. He was worse he was the same he was worse he was worse he would never be better.

Such a fool, he said, naïve. The line is broken it is broken it is gone. They have won. That is it. They have won. I was from the moon but I will never go home again. I am there no longer I do not know where I will be, just dirt, for a while, just dirt. It's all I am it's all I'm worth. Poor fool, deluded, a life of delusion. What can you do what can you be when all is delusion.

I did not know, I could not answer him he was not looking for an answer, his brain, his body, their unity in failure, his magic, their collapse.

It was not always so, there were days of plans, of fruitfulness, the fruitfulness so painful, I gobbled it up, all I could, all I could while I could, his mind, his ways, I adored him, I adore him.

What I would like now, Jerry said another time, is a glass of wine and some cheese that oozes. I do not know its name but I know that it is creamy and tangy and that it oozes. I never made cheese, isn't that a crime. I never became a farmer I should have been a farmer can't you just picture it. What did I become instead oh yes an international whore. How would I like to spend my final two decades because really I doubt I will live much more than 69, what do you think my dear Gareth.

Gareth was visiting, he did often, would sit with me and Jerry, sometimes took over so I could go and get food, go for a walk, go, before I returned.

I think you'll make it to 73, said Gareth, Gareth was crying as he spoke, the tears not causing his voice to break, he had become used to crying and speaking.

I will live until I am 73 at least, said Jerry. Soon I will have the keys to our farm. Gareth will you come and live with us.

How won-der-ful, said Gareth, my every dream fulfilled, to live within the stink of shit.

Your natural environment, said Jerry. Give me my pencil and some paper.

Jerry drew. He started with a farmhouse, It will be generous, he said, rooms and rooms so that people can stay and stay and stay and they can work if they like or not work it is their choice.

Jerry drew a garden, he spent time drawing his garden, we watched him, we watched him in this time, his time, the time he made for himself by imagining what he could never have, time while his brain could still conceive of time, Jerry's skin sinking and sinking in, his disappearance, still present but gone, just to stay here in this horror, I remember thinking, just to pause and to stop and to stay here in this horror.

Barns, said Jerry, for parties, for people, they can do what they want, they can gather, they can discuss, they can make films, make art, show films, show art, performance, can you pass me the water Gareth,

Gareth passed Jerry the glass with water, a straw, Jerry tried to drink, he could not drink, the weight on him of futility, the burden, his disappointment in himself, his shame, his humiliation, his terror, his grief for himself, the loss of himself, losing himself as he watched, as we watched, he lay back, he rested, he said nothing we said nothing, his breath rattled. Awake asleep it was the same.

Where is my drawing, said Jerry, time had passed who knows how much time, little or much, all the same.

The vegetable garden, said Jerry, we will be self-sufficient. We will grow and we will store and we shall have all we need and any excess we can sell and pay for the farm and pay for our lives it will all work in cycles it will be cycles it will be life.

You want to recreate what we had in the warehouses, said Gareth.

Not recreate, said Jerry, it is regrowth. New new new. Never pastiche, never the same, new.

Jerry kept drawing, his vegetable garden growing and growing, all sense of scale shot, he drew stars he drew spirals he drew a helter skelter he drew a rollercoaster. And then from it he started to draw lines, and then a line that went to the edge of the page. Jerry took a new sheet and continued a line, the line horizontal across the bottom, one edge to the other, a horizon line, land. He drew a new line, off-centre, on a tight diagonal, from the horizon line up to two thirds of the page, like the line was leaning to the left. At the top of the line, Jerry drew a large circle, like a sun or a moon, or the cycle of living, the wholeness, it was as if the line was leaning on the circle, that if the circle were to move, the line would falter and fall and it would fall for ever and it would be gone.

I need to get rid of the darkness, said Jerry. I asked him what he meant. He grasped at the air to the right of him. The darkness here, he said. This darkness, if I can just get rid of it.

The room was bright, summer light high and unrelenting, it's over there, it's always over there. If I can just get my focus that is all I need.

Gareth was gripping Jerry's hand, I was crying and crying, My love, said Jerry, I love you more than the world.

Gareth looked at me Gareth tried to smile mouth closed it wasn't a smile it was emotion sadness love. Gareth said to me, come and sit here Johnny, and he stood and kissed Jerry on the forehead, what had been his forehead, now skin stretched over skull, I took Jerry's hand I sat down, Gareth was weeping he kissed me on the head, on my hair, he left us, I'm here Jerry, I said, I was gripping his hand, Jerry was trying to smile I know his face, I know his smile it was there.

Johnny you are the love of my life, said Jerry. He could barely say the words, he wanted to cry he couldn't cry. You are my great love my only love in my life that has been full of love, my life has been for love. Thank you Johnny.

I now know love, I said, or something like it, words like it, I did not know love and I may have never known love, not the love that you have shown me, that you show me. I love you Jerry, I will love you always.

You must continue, said Jerry. He paused. To love, or all is lost, do not lose it, live for love, live with love, fight for love, welcome love, accept love, embrace love, love in this hell. It is all I can give you Johnny it is everything you have given me. I'm so scared for you Johnny I'm so scared please forgive me.

I could not console him.

I love you, I said to him, I love you I love you I love you, I was gripping his hand kissing his hand gripping his hand, Jerry was inconsolable, crying without crying, pushing out on a hard ledge high alone in a storm, stuck in this bed in this room, all around others stuck in their bed in their room, in their own inconsolable peril, Jerry was moaning, pain present and urgent, words went, there was no time for words, no time for their complications, their finessing, their corners and paths, Jerry a master of words, now those words evaporated, energy needed elsewhere, focus, Jerry's focus on his pain, unremitting intensity, he could only moan and wince and gasp for air and then cease, rest was not the word for it, there was no rest, pain had merely relented for a while, maybe minutes maybe hours, so began days of it, days of pain, communication beyond words, his body dysfunctional, he would stir and he would flinch and he would moan, pain present again, his body no longer his body, his body was pain, no difference, It's OK Jerry, it's OK, I would say, words like it, useless words, it was not OK it would not be OK, others who loved Jerry in the room with me others who loved Jerry not in the room with me, days and days, visitors sometimes other times us alone, Jerry sometimes able to acknowledge a visitor's presence, sometimes, a nod of the head to himself, a look as if he were saying hello within, no words came, confusion then on Jerry's face when there was no response, Jerry returning to the conversation in his head, conversing with pain, he would cease, not rest, still rattling with breath, still alive, motionless, he would stir and moan and I would say or someone would say, Jerry, hello Jerry, I'm here, it's OK, as if there were some hope, there was no hope, Jerry kept in purgatory, trying and trying, focusing and focusing, to rid himself of the pain that had become his body, it was not a body it was pain. I would say to him over and over, it's OK Jerry, it's OK, when it was not OK, it was not OK, and then Jerry stirred and Jerry moaned and Jerry writhed, his body true pain, it was not OK, it was never going to be OK, and I held Jerry's hand and I said to Jerry, You can rest, Jerry, you can rest.

    Silence of tears, they fell from my eyes but my voice

stayed calm, Jerry did not know of my tears Jerry heard my calm, he calmed. Jerry would cease, and then time after time, some time or no time, Jerry would stir and moan and again I would say, you can rest, you can rest, this was truth I was not lying I no longer said, It's OK, it was not OK. I said truth I said, You can rest. I said, I love you Jerry, I said, I love you. The nurse said, we can set a cot up in the room for you, you can be here tonight, and so I stayed with Jerry, I stayed, me and my love, I love you Jerry, you can rest, I love you Jerry, you can rest, it was 1am, 2am, I was gone, he was breathing, immovable, breathing, I kissed Jerry on his lips of sores, those lips that I had kissed so many times before those lips of love, through which had come his words of love. I went to the cot I lay down, I don't know if I slept but I was asleep. I woke and I knew, I knew before I stood, Jerry was gone. I wept and I went to Jerry and I wept and Jerry was gone I sat with Jerry and Jerry was gone. I called the nurse the nurse came Jerry was gone. The nurse consoled me and Jerry was gone. The nurse brought me tea and Jerry was gone. The nurse let me sit with Jerry I sat with Jerry and Jerry was gone. I sat and I sat and then I asked the nurse if I could use the phone. I dialled Gareth's number, Gareth picked up after two rings, I said Jerry's gone, I wept, it was all I could say. Gareth wept Gareth said he would come straight away. The nurse let me sit with Jerry then Gareth came and Gareth sat with me and Jerry was gone. We talked of Jerry and Jerry was gone. Doctors came to record Jerry's death and Jerry was gone. We said goodbye to Jerry but Jerry was gone and we said goodbye and Gareth drove me to his home it was a Thursday I remember July 20th 1995.

13

Time deadened. I did not know time. Gareth looked out for me, Gareth cared. How are you, I was asked, or, are you OK, what could I say, the loss, the violence, the waves, the pull, the surges, the deadening.

The funeral happened it was for others not for me, I was there but I was not there. I was told the funeral will help, it did not help. Others organized it, others spoke at it, I was there but not there, his body was burned, Jerry's wishes. There was a gathering, it turned into a party, Jerry's wishes. I was there but not there.

I lived in Jerry's home without Jerry. Weeks passed. I needed to get out I did not know anything what was I meant to do, work? All that I knew, how could they ever know. I did not want to see anybody I did not want to know anybody I did not want sympathy I did not want questions I did not want any of it I wanted Jerry. Gareth booked me a plane ticket Gareth organized me a place to stay I was gone.

I had never flown before, I had no idea. I packed a kit bag I got to the airport deadened mush weight I was hours early. I queued and I queued and it was like the plane was going to leave I would miss it it would be gone.

I got to the front I handed in my ticket I got my boarding

pass. Seat 56A. I was alone there was no Jerry I was alone. I was so early there was so much time time was dead. What was I meant to do where was I meant to go. There were magazines there were books there were newspapers I did not want magazines I did not want books I did not want newspapers I did not want to know. There were chairs I sat in a chair. Lines of chairs, bolted to the floor. Nothing could move nothing could change. Permanent stasis. There was a screen it showed the flights it showed the times it showed the status it showed the gate. I stared at the screen I panicked where was the information would I miss it. If I stared could I make the information come. I stared and I stared, other flights boarded other flights closed, the planes disappeared, no information for my flight, no information, it didn't exist, I didn't exist.

    The flight was called. Go to gate 23. I got to the gate as quick as I could, panicked, it will go without me. Got to the gate, people and people and people, nothing. More chairs and chairs, not enough for the people, another screen, I found some space by a wall, I crouched down I sat on the floor, this was my spot. A day of waiting, the administration of time, time deadened, I was at home in this no-time time, I could have stayed there in that state and it would be it and that would be that.

    Boarding was called, I stood, I queued, I waited, no order, order. I got on the plane, my first plane, I got to my seat, more waiting, no time, time. Two wedged in next to me, felt wedged in, I had the window. An announcement, the plane was fully boarded. Another announcement. Another. A safety demonstration. I was going to die who cared. The time we were meant to leave came and went. The plane moved. It moved and then it did not move. We stayed in the same place. This was life, motionless. That's how I saw it that's how I felt. The plane moved we were going nowhere. The plane moved the plane moved an announcement, cabin crew please take your seats, the plane moved the plane moved the plane stopped and pivoted. Engines fired body pushed back pressure speed release forward and up unbodied hard high pressure it's what I needed the engine cut out we were going to die. Out of the window houses, roads, a reservoir, a castle, a flag raised high, the plane turning over the castle we were going to crash into the castle, the engine cut out, we were going to die, engine kicked in, upwards, onwards, on.

    The plane shook and it was broken in pieces. The plane flew on. The plane broke into clouds the pilots couldn't see we were going to crash into another plane and another and another. The plane broke through clouds up and beyond another world. Nothing happened.

    Gareth had given me a notebook, he said write so I wrote, this is how it was, over some hours, stopping, starting, stopping, writing.

THIS SUN. It does not set it does not set. It just stays and stays. I wish Jerry could see. Primal up here. I am scared. This tin that I am in, feels like it could snap and break right now right here up here.

    It makes you think. This world has been this world since for ever, nothing new is ever created, the same atoms always reconfigured, I have always been in it, Jerry has always been in it, in other forms, reframed, re-amalgamated.

The sun does not set, yet the sky is trying to be night. One star up there, alone, deep depth dark on high, grading down through blues, a sunset, except the sun is not setting it is staying the same, what is a sunset if the sun does not set. Plane is so weird smokers at the back smoking. No food no drink. There are attendants with trolleys they are so far away they are so slow they will never come. The plane full. Whoever is in front of me, whoever is behind me, they have closed their windows. So weird. The outside they do not want to know.

Food came drink came I ate it I drank it I need more drink how do I get more. No one comes. No one comes. They come. More wine. The sun not set and still it does not set.

It does not set.

It sets.

The light, the glow, the colour, the change, lines.

IT IS JERRY'S PAINTINGS.

It's Jerry's fucking paintings up here in this sky this is what he was painting. It's Jerry up here, up here always. The line, the colour, or at least what we call colour, Jerry would say all the time, colour doesn't exist, just like we don't exist, not in any real way, just matter swirling about, forming, reforming, I miss him.

A line of cloud close is wisping. A line of dark against dark, this depth, this darkness, matter, that's all there is, Jerry called it a cosmic joke, the magnitude, the nothingness, if Jerry was here sat with me now he would be saying it was a cosmic joke, but his eyes would have been saying, there is no joke, if those eyes were next to me now.

I've been crying I'm always crying. It's what I do I cry. The attendant said to me are you OK, what could I say? I couldn't say. The attendant gave me more wine.

It still goes on. My watch says its 19.14 but what does that mean. It is all breaking down now, it is right, it should happen. I will try and write it. Darkness of lines blurring, to become just darkness. Then the darkness breaks and there is light again, but then the darkness blurs to become darkness again, these graded bands, it's like a dark rainbow, a rainbow of darkness. It is another of Jerry's paintings. He saw it.

Blurred darkness, just light behind, light as if no colour, but there is a line of orange it is like a crack in the sky. Far in the distance. A line like a seam. So intense. Darkness, orange seam, darkness, that's all there is. Wait I've just looked back behind the colour is still wild back there. Sunset still held, it's like everything always now is the end, this emptiness, this fullness.

The intensity of nothing. It is now beyond colour, this colour, why do we need to name it why do we need to explain. What is this colour is this where colour goes of course it goes nowhere it does not exist. So dark so suddenly, blurring is taking over, darkness darkness then a veiled burst, like far off on a murky horizon, to me it is a blur but where it is whatever it is it is power. Now just darkness now just darkness and a band of serenity between, a band of acceptance, jade, but blurred, it is another of Jerry's paintings, did he ever see this did he ever fly like this, at this time, in this permanent sunset, or did Jerry just see and if Jerry could see then can I see. Can I see. Can I.

It was all I wrote. I still have the notebook, its first few pages filled, the rest empty, the attendant took pity on me, kept giving me more and more wine. It was dark, what could I do, there was a film, I had no interest in the film, no choice, just one film shown to everyone all at the same time, screens from the ceiling in the aisles every few rows. I tried to sleep but sleep did not come. The film ended there were no more films in place of the film was a map.

The plane was approaching land. The plane shook. It was horror. It shook. Horror. I remember thinking, this was it. I watched the map. The plane was over a place called Newfoundland. As it flew, as minutes passed, the names of other places popped up. And then there it was. Nova Scotia. We were flying right over Nova Scotia. I was home. Jerry was here. Nova Scotia right below me. I could fall right here dropped down dead and I would have been happy. Home was here. Jerry was here.

What was this Nova Scotia, I had never thought what Nova Scotia was, it was island, it was land, it was place. Was it always its name, why was it given its name, what had it been before? Why was our block Nova Scotia what was the connection why names. Out the window, sometimes breaks in cloud, sometimes clusters of lights on land below. On the map town names: Halifax, New Glasgow, what is this world, Windsor. I took out a cassette, I put on a cassette, I put on my headphones, it played. The Cure, 'Close To Me'.

It went on. There was an announcement about forms, we had to fill in forms, they would bring round forms. No one brought round forms they brought round forms. My name,

Jonathan Grant, my address, 1 Nova Scotia House. It went on it went on. And then there were questions: have you ever been convicted of an offence? No. Have you ever been involved in espionage or in terrorist activities or genocide? No. Are you HIV positive?

What were they asking why were they asking? It said: if you have answered yes to any of the above you may be refused admission.

The plane crashed it broke apart the shock the horror. Jerry would have been refused admission Jerry would have been banned I was going somewhere where Jerry was banned. I was going there I could not stop I was going for solace I was going to escape and instead I was going to a hell.

I asked, could I not fill out the form. I had to fill out the form. I ticked no I ticked no I ticked no how dare they. The plane descended the plane landed how dare they. Off the plane down a corridor how dare they. I queued and I queued a lifetime of queueing how dare they. Passport check hand in my form I was ready I was going to say how dare they. It was my turn I handed over my passport I handed over my form the officer stared at me the officer read my form I was terrified I said nothing. The officer said, you here for work or pleasure, Gareth told me to say pleasure I said pleasure I lied and I lied and I lied.

Gareth had given me money for a taxi, I told the driver the address on E10th St. We drove. My body not my own awake asleep what was I. The drive was wild so fast so lawless. I was asleep I was awake asleep the driver so fast the drive took for ever. There is the city there it is, Jerry never saw it he always wanted to see it he never made it here I am here for him I am here without him. The emptiness the loneliness what was this. Over a bridge there was the city I was in the city. Streets a grid, the taxi juddered and juddered and drove wild and juddered, everyone everywhere, couldn't believe I was there, I was there, I did not want to be there did not want to be anywhere.

The cab dropped me at the address. I paid. The key was meant to be under the mat I looked under the mat I couldn't see the key. I had nowhere to stay. I looked and there was a second mat and the key was under the mat. Keys were weird they did not work I made them work. The apartment so weird so old so poky, so hot, a radiator burning hot, it hissed, I could not turn it down, I was awake I was asleep what was it, nine? I got the keys I went out on the street.

A skeleton walked towards me, another, two more. Three skeletons overtook me. Skeleton faces, painted, some with flowers in their hair, some with costumes elaborate, what was this place, skeletons everywhere. At the corner across the road a church on a diagonal, skeletons flooding it, I followed the skeletons, they sucked me in, skeletons and community, a banner tied up,

DAY OF THE DEAD
22ND ANNUAL FESTIVAL
ART MAKING *LIVE MUSIC*
COMMEMORATION

Was this a joke I had come to escape death I had landed among the dead. I bristled I was repelled, a tidal pull away, yet I stayed. A skeleton caught my eye a skeleton smiled at me, a skeleton said, would you like to commemorate a loved one you have lost?

How dare they. I stared I said nothing. How did they know what did they know. And yet I broke, I was broken. I cried, I couldn't speak, I did not know where I was I did not know when I was I did not know what I was I just knew I was lost I just knew I had lost Jerry. The skeleton asked if they could hug me, I managed to nod my head I managed to make a noise.

Do you have a photo, said a skeleton, I shook my head, I could not speak. You can write their name here, a skeleton gave me a card, you can place it on the altar.

Jerry did not believe in religion Jerry hated religion but this was different this was skeletons I wrote on the card in big letters J E R R Y F I E L D and a heart. Placed it on the altar. I cried and I cried and a skeleton said, it's OK, it's OK, but it was not OK.

I lit a candle, I cried, I do not know how long I cried, I was asleep, awake, I cried. Someone meant something to somebody, someone said, I turned to look, he did not exist. His jaw his height his hair long but cropped, his size his smile his eyes, impossible, he did not exist, he did not exist he was here he was talking to me.

I said something like what, some sort of a word, more a noise, more a mumble, and he said, it's OK. I said, I'm sorry, I said, all over the place. I said again, sorry. He said, when will you people stop apologizing.

He held out his hand he said his name was Derek. I shook his hand his handshake was impossible. He said let's get out of here, he said, I'm done with death, he said, let's go get a drink, he said, sounds good?

We walked a few blocks, turned right, I'd been in the city

what less than an hour and already been picked up by a guy, Jerry always said I could get picked up at a funeral I mean he was nearly right, what was I going to do what could I do. An awning out into the street, security on the door, security asked for ID, I showed my passport. What was this place, like a downstairs room of a house, I mean really it was not a pub it was so weird, like a massive downstairs, emboldened scared who cares, so busy, all those humans, everyone everywhere, they filled the space, in each other's space, Derek knew everybody, everybody was impossible, sex and sex and sex, sex present in the room, I was used to furtiveness at home, everybody overt here, Derek bought me a beer I drank the beer, Derek bought me another he was talking to everyone he introduced me to everyone it was impossible I was gone in a second, jetlag, I couldn't talk my head was nodding I was at sea in impossibility, I was drunk but had barely drunk anything, Derek said, are you OK, Derek said, I'll get you home, Derek said, where are you staying. Derek walked me to the corner of the block really I was a mess. Derek said what are you doing tomorrow I said nothing. Derek said meet me at two and he said the name of a coffee place and he kissed me on the lips Derek kissed me impossibility kissed me.

    I got into the apartment the radiator hissed it was so hot it was 23.41 I could have slept a century. I woke up after I'd slept a century it was 3.07. Tried to sleep tried to sleep lay awake made it to 5.32. I was awake and I was awake. The radiator hissed I had to get out. Still dark. Across the road down the end of the block a diner, in its window a neon that said *WE NEVER CLOSE* *OPEN 24/7* *24h*.

Skeletons at a table, still up from the night before. A skeleton at a table, on his own, flesh nearly gone, staring off somewhere, cigarette in his hand he did not bring it to his lips, no one with him, maybe he wanted no one with him, he saw me looking he did not look at me, a coffee in front of him his other hand on the cup, he did not lift up the cup he did not move it maybe he just liked its warmth.

    Just for one sir, a waiter said to me, had I been a sir before, was I now a sir. I said yes, the waiter said, seat at the bar. A bar, bar stools fixed to the floor, the bar in front of an open kitchen, a griddle, burners, ingredients, three cooks, so glamorous, I was so hungry, I was still drunk, or jet-lagged, both, ordered scrambled eggs potato pancakes corn beef hash, you want coffee, the waiter said, I said yes, you want juice, I said yes, it was good to say yes it was what I needed.

    It was what I needed, these people, this openness, this possibility, this life in the dark. Coffee came it was good, food came it was impossible, there was a newspaper I read it, night became dawn and this morning light made me close to Jerry.

Light and light and light. The city took me out of myself. 2pm met Derek at the coffee place he was impossible and he smiled and it was impossible. My tender friend, he called me, I was his friend already I didn't yet realize that charm could be brazen. Derek said he worked in a gallery had I heard of it? I hadn't. The gallery had just opened its new space purpose built had I heard about it? I hadn't. It's closed today I'll take you there when it's open, he said. I said, OK.

His impossibility in daylight was more possible, his face's asymmetry clearer, everyone is wonky, everyone knows everyone else is wonky, why try and hide it, but his hands so big, body so broad, hair a curtain to be pulled back, which he did, repeatedly, an effect, smile so beguiling, smile so trained.

Who made you cry, said Derek, and then he said, yesterday, in the church. And so I told him about Jerry and I told him and I told him and he would say fuck or no or I'm so sorry and then he said, you want another coffee?

I told him and I told him and I cried.

And how are you, he said. I looked at him like, it's pretty clear, and then he said, your health I mean. And I said, oh, and I said, I'm fine, and I said, I'm OK, and the words felt like a judgement on Jerry but I didn't know how else to say them. I'm glad, he said, he drank his coffee, he said, I know what, I want to go see this show. Derek said the name of the artist, have you heard of him? I hadn't. Derek said, he's an HIV positive artist. Derek said, it might help you.

I did not want to be helped I did not want help. But it was this city it was Derek he was impossible so I said, sure.

We finished our coffee we walked some streets so straight so strange. I was in a daze I did not want to go I was going. This is it, he said, we were at a door in a building on a street that was so long it was like it went to a horizon. We went in we went upstairs Derek bought me a ticket we went into the exhibition, up the corner of the first room a pile of sweets. You can take one, said Derek, when you take a sweet from the pile I think it's like watching someone waste away. I took a sweet it was like I was taking from Jerry.

Two clocks were on a wall, touching, almost telling the same time, almost ticking at the same time. Lightbulbs on a string came from the ceiling then pooled on the floor. Words went around the top of a room. It was like Jerry I didn't understand how it was like Jerry it was nothing like Jerry it was like Jerry.

We separated in the space, going at our own pace, I didn't want it explaining I wanted to feel it, that was how I'd always been with Jerry, how he'd been with me, that is how we looked at art. In a room there was just a platform, pale blue almost grey, lightbulbs lining its perimeter on the top, that's all there was in the room that's what it was. I stared at the podium I stared, I was there for an age and I stared. An impossible guy walked into the room muscled he just wore tiny silver tight shorts, trainers he was impossible, he didn't look at me, he had on headphones he carried a Walkman, he didn't look at me he climbed on the podium he started dancing he didn't look at me. I couldn't hear what music he was dancing to he didn't look at me I stared at him I stared. He danced he danced, his dance like he was somewhere else sometime else and all was OK or maybe all was not OK and all there was for him to do was dance, that nothing was OK really nothing, nothing was OK ever, and all he could do was dance, he was so impossible and he was here and he danced and he danced and he danced. The room was silent but in his ears was music and it's all he needed, to help him be in this horror to help him. It was adult and I did not understand and I understood. I was crying and I was crying. He danced and he danced and then he stopped and he walked off and no one else saw no one it was just me and him but to him it was just himself he didn't acknowledge me at all. He left and I was left there and I stared at the podium I wiped my face I wiped my tears and I stared at the podium I don't know how long. Derek came into the room and he came close to me and he said, this is a performance work, a dancer dances for a few minutes everyday but they don't announce when, most of the day it's just the podium unless you get lucky.

    I asked him, did you ever get lucky, and he smiled at me and winked and said, never.

    I knew what I wanted I knew how to get it, I wanted it and I wanted it now, I wanted Derek to fuck me, impossible man in this impossible city, break everything destroy everything just fuck, but that's all I wanted I didn't want a lover I didn't want to start anything I just wanted to be fucked by the impossible. And so I did what I had to do, I charmed him, me the naïve young thing new to the city, show me things, we walked, he guided, oh wow how beautiful, the city, a building, another building, this park, that view, oh wow, this cocktail, this food, oh wow, another drink, sure, edging closer and closer the whole time, our bodies accidentally on purpose touching the whole time, it was clear the path we were on, and then we kissed and then Derek said, do you want to come back to mine, and so the path was the path.

    We got to his place, went upstairs how many more stairs, it was kind of broke it was kind of busted. He said, do you want a drink, and so we went into the kitchen and in the kitchen was a bathtub.

    Old buildings, he said, tenement, he said, can't be changed, he said, what can you do. He passed me a beer I put my hand up his shirt he pulled me in my hand went round his back, impossible and warm and broad and hot,

my hand went down into his jeans my hand went under his
boxers his arse hard and big and impossible, all this muscle
what was its purpose. My first guy since Jerry died and I bit
him. He got me to his bedroom he got me naked he got his
cock down my throat he wasn't impossible, but it was good.
It was good it was normal it was hard and he was insistent
we made out more his jaw his body still impossible his cock
normal you cannot hide. He was fingering my arse he was
kissing me he had got me he knew what he was doing his
fingers deep. His body on me his mouth by my ear he was
saying stuff he was saying stuff and his cock was at my
hole and he was pressing and he was pressing it like one
more push and he would be in. Can I fuck you, he said, and,
is it OK, and he was pressing and he was pressing, and I
made noises like yes and he pressed a little harder like it
was almost in and then the tip was in he was just inside me
and he groaned and he said oh fuck and he said so good
and he said I want you and he said is it OK and he said I'm
clean and he said I like it raw.

   And in that moment, that moment of relent, the body
relents, the mind relents, I relented all of me, worry about it
later, override worry, fly high up over above worry into
impossibility, relent relent relent, relent like a surge of
hormone, and so I made a noise like an affirmative and I
loosened my body I let him in this impossible man and his
normal cock and he fucked me, then he fucked me
again, then we slept, and I dreamt of Jerry, running ahead of
me, running and running, into a black space, never looking
back, running and running and running. I woke before dawn
I got up I had cum dripping from my arse I found my clothes
I put them on. He stirred he said what are you doing, he

said, come back to bed. I said something like, I've got to make a call home, I said, the time difference. I said something about my bank. He said OK, he said meet me at 10, same place. I said sure and I fled and at 10 I was as far away as I could be.

Worry was in me straight away, the worry and the worry and the worry, what had I done, what had I done. I worried and I worried and maybe it was what I wanted, that burden, that fear.

14

I do not know what to do I do not know what I want. It is 7.21am. The light will come in through the front window it will hit Jerry's painting and then it will go up and will go over and it will be blocked. I do not want to be here. I do not want to be here any more I have nowhere to go.

It is still low it is only February it has little power it has power. I used to love this soil when there's nothing. It's all there under the soil, in the soil, waiting to happen, waiting for light, but now the tower is built the light is blocked the light will not come it will never come.

I did it last night I messaged that guy. He's in my phone as BRIDGE GUY I should have him in my phone as ASSHOLE. There was nothing going on there was nothing happening no one responding, I couldn't deal with the nothing I needed to do something. Hey, I messaged, what are you up to.

He didn't see it he saw it he read it he didn't reply. He didn't reply he replied. He was writing something, it appeared: Hello stranger, and then, oh now you want it.

Wait when we'd last messaged he hadn't got back to me the asshole. But I wanted it now so just play along what's the point in being pedantic.

Ha, I wrote, yeah, I wrote.

Come over then, he wrote, watching a film, he wrote, you can try and distract me.

I douched. I got out the flat I got over there the shop at the bottom of his block boarded up no more convenience.

He messaged me the code for the door, for the lift, it smelt the same it was always the same. I found the door I rang its bell, he opened it he said, you finally bothered.

I didn't care I wasn't there for counselling I was there to fuck. I went to kiss him but he said easy, wait a minute. He went into his lounge there was a stepladder by the windows windows windows. He climbed up he attached a drape he climbed down he moved the step ladder he attached a drape. He said, blinds are broken.

He walked to his bedroom, let's watch the movie, he said, he got on the bed, the screen as big as the room was frozen on an image, one actor looking off to the middle distance, another actor looking at the actor looking off to the middle distance.

I'd seen the film already it was awful. It was about two guys going on at each other about finding love and not finding love, how no one understood them and would they ever find their place in the world and they just wanted to be normal.

Let's play Mr and Mrs, said the guy whose name I didn't know, patting the other side of the bed.

Who's Mrs, I said.

Like you have to ask, he said.

I took off my shoes I climbed over him I draped myself on him my head on his shoulder I mean I may as well try. He pressed play on the remote the actors started saying their lines it was so loud.

I just want to live a normal life, the character continued, to be loved, just like anyone, he said.

Ohmygod this film, said the guy whose name I did not know, it's like this film is speaking to my soul.

Yeah, I said but really I was staring at his crotch. My hand was on his stomach I moved my hand down I slid my hand down under his joggers I mean what were we here for.

You're so desperate, said the guy whose name I didn't know, but he didn't do anything to stop me. The film went on. Other stuff happened. I played with his cock I played with his balls, the usual, I got him hard I knew what I was doing.

One of the actors playing one of the characters said, yeah why should being gay be any different.

The screen froze. The guy whose name I didn't know had the remote held out high, he'd pressed pause, he wanted me to see he'd pressed pause, the performance had begun. Do you take anything seriously, he said. At your age, he said.

What could I say, that I thought the film he loved was peddling fear, fear of difference fear of individuality fear of what is unknown. I wanted him to fuck me if I said the film he loved was peddling fear he might not want to fuck me I didn't say the film he loved was peddling fear.

I had his cock out of his joggers I was banging it against his stomach. OK you're going to get it, he said, and then I was on him he was on me and it was on. Except it wasn't on it was a performance of being on it was nothing like before it was nothing real. I wasn't just drunk before I wasn't imagining it, before it was good it was so good. But now there was no tease there was no play there was no battle. There was no engagement there were no smiles there was no conspiracy nothing was being made. Can I film it he said I said sure I mean who cares.

What does he want, other than what he thinks he wants. How far is he from wanting nothing. How far am I from wanting nothing. I am so far but that guy, fucking me without looking at me, looking at his phone at footage of him fucking me, the two actors frozen on the screen behind me frozen in state of being paid to pretend they are experiencing love, his cock in my arse his left hand holding my right leg his left hand holding his phone, his phone angled pretty flat down I mean he had no interest in filming my face he had no interest in filming my cock I mean it must have been in his shot but he never mentioned it he never jerked it. His camera was flat down he was peering into it oh yeah he was saying, I am destroying you hole, that's what he said, or things like that, fucking ruining you, he said, he wasn't, meanwhile his left hand just held my leg his cock just went in and out he was so boring. He held his phone that was it oh I'm going to cum I'm going to cum I mean please get on with it. I came, he came.

Oh fuck, he said, like he'd actually done something, like something had happened, like what he had done mattered.

He on his back me on my back. I went over to hold him he said, gross. I said what do you mean, he said, dripping with cum, he said, cleaner just changed the sheets, he said, you're a fucking mess.

I mean he was right. I was a mess I am a mess so what. But what was he, so clean, so empty, his mean bedroom, mean space, no room to move, that slit of a window, bed filling the space, no air, this human confined, his desire contained, this is what he wanted, luxury it is called, there we lay barren in luxury.

I wanted more I wanted to keep going why not. Come on, I said. No, he said. If you don't mind, he said. I need to call it a night, he said. Early conference call, he said. I want to sleep alone, he said. Read the room, he said.

What was I doing why did I bother why put myself in that state. I was going to leave anyway, I said, though I'd no plans either way I didn't care. What I wanted was a fuck and what I wanted was camaraderie the two can be the same the two can be symbiotic even if it's an anonymous fuck even if it's fleeting even if you never know the guy there is still camaraderie it's there it can be there that is the point. What have I lost why have I lost it can I get it back. I mean not with this guy he's not my project. Whatever was hot about him before he's lost it it's gone. He's trimmer he's fitter he's neater it's gone.

Where's the remote, he said. I got up I was getting dressed, you don't want to shower, he said, no, I said, I'm a mess. Here it is, he said, talking to himself, acting like I wasn't there, I'd fulfilled my purpose, he pressed play, why should it even matter that we're men, said one of the characters, I was putting on my pants I had the cum of that guy dripping out my arse I didn't care. I hate that word queer, said one of the characters, I'm a gay man why do I want to be queer, when I was a kid queer was an insult why would I call myself queer now, I want to live in a world where there is no need for labels.

Queer queer queer queer queer queer, that's what was going through my head. Queer queer queer queer queer queer.

I hate men who call themselves queer, said the guy whose name I did not know, his cock in his hand, it was soft, holding it like a safety blanket. Grow up, be a man, said the guy whose name I didn't know.

Our love is the same, said one of the characters, straight or gay there is no difference, said one of the characters, oh god, said the guy whose name I didn't know, this film gets me every time, he said, I couldn't find my jeans, I found my jeans, I put on my jeans, our love is universal, said one of the characters, we will live for ever in our love, the actor playing the character was making himself cry, making himself cry while he told lies, facile lies of love and for ever and love never dying and other lies humans say to avoid the way things are how things really are, the lie of normality, it's what Jerry ran from it's what I run from, the trap, it's still there, it renews, it takes new forms, it's happening again, hold me, said one of actors acting as one the characters, hold me like this is for ever.

The guy whose name I didn't know was sobbing, his chest heaving, gets me every time, he said, holding his soft cock, he did not look at me he looked at the screen he did not look at me he looked at his phone. He looked at his phone he looked at his phone he put his phone down he looked at the screen he did not look at me.

OK I'm going, I said, he said nothing, then he said, wait it's almost the end, then one of the characters said, I will never let you go, for all time.

The guy whose name I didn't know was inconsolable. Bye, I said, he said, don't steal anything. I went out the bedroom I closed the door it closed with a swoosh. The drape he had hung up had half fallen down. In the opposite apartment the lights were on full. There was a sofa just like his sofa. There was a guy on the sofa staring at something it must have been a screen he was wearing a sweatshirt sweatpants his hand down his sweatpants his hand on his cock he was staring at the screen. He did not see me I went and stood right by the window right across from him he did not see me. I went to leave and went past the sofa of the guy whose name I did not know, his precious sofa, I went over to it I pulled down my trousers I pulled down my pants I sat I wiped my arse on his couch I wiped my arse and whatever was coming out of it.

Why do I do it to myself why do I go there what more proof do I need what do I want these men to be what approval am I seeking did Jerry seek this approval did Jerry need something did Jerry want validation. What was he trying to heal. Or was he so cut off from his past, so propelled by rejection, that really it was fuel to him. Because really we are talking about daddy issues, we all know it, it's obvious, we still cannot face it, not just daddy issues, our daddy's issues with their daddy, a daddy's daddy's issues with their daddy, it goes on, it's relentless. I am stuck in my daddy issues Jerry was propelled by them Jerry pushed away. Jerry hated normal he would have hated that guy whose name I did not know he would have loved hearing about him. You have a magnetic pull to awfulness, he would say.

So how come I'm with you, I'd say.

Jerry would say, I'm the worst.

What am I going to do where am I going to go. I do not want this place to be this sad place. I have stayed here because it worked and now it will not work. All my life as an adult all I have known is a place to live that works. We grew we cooked we shared we lived. And then I lost Jerry. And then I grew I cooked I lived. Living is home is a home that works is a home that is intuitive. This was available this was possible now it is not possible. Stay here in shade I cannot grow what do I do, buy all my food? What with?

What is this place why am I here what can I do. It's like this flat is Jerry and Jerry is this flat but he got this place by chance no one else wanted it no one else cared. It was never his it was never ours it is not mine do not become sentimental do not become trapped.

It's been good but now it's not good maybe it's not been good for a while maybe I've been fooling myself. What was working doesn't work. What do you do when things don't work. Change. How do I change. I don't know. I could stay here I could stay here at least until Jerry's sister dies and then the game is up I'm out I have no rights I'm not even meant to be here. She is 72 now she could live another twenty years so awful to be reliant on another's survival. I am not worthy of a home. I am worthy of a home if I can afford a home I cannot afford a home. What do I do. I help the sick, or at least I try to. I am not worthy of a home. It's so banal, it's so normal, is this the normal that the guy whose name I do not know wants? Probably. I can stay here in Jerry's world, our world, my world, but it is now our world because now there is no light. If there had not been light Jerry would not have stayed Jerry would not have made it his home, back then, back when Jerry was first offered the place, when no one wanted it, when the council offered them to queers, the council that no longer exists. The new block blocking the light, its apartments called luxury, as luxurious as the apartment of the guy whose name I do not know. I cannot grow I cannot live there is no place for me here. Jerry would not have stayed Jerry would feel no ties, are you kidding, he would have said, get the fuck out. Do not dwell. Do not be their experiment, be your own.

I do not want to go I do not want to go. I should go. I do not want to face it I can't deal. The quilt is on display again it's the second time they've put it on display since they got it out of storage the first time I couldn't go I just couldn't go. Friends went Gareth went I couldn't go. Today is the last day then it will be put away again I should go I cannot go.

We tried to quilt a panel for Jerry we tried. We started, Gareth and Fiona and I, we wanted to quilt a garden but somehow also make it the wildest party. None of us had sewn before, we were too ambitious, we wanted it to be everything, we couldn't get anywhere, we tried, we tried. Then things happened life moved in the way that life moved, it wasn't forwards, it was like circumnavigating, that's how grief was for me, how grief is for me, circumnavigation, always going round, circularity is what I want anyway who wants forwards, the guy whose name I cannot remember, he would want forwards, progress, a lie.

Life moved in its circular way and we didn't finish the panel we couldn't finish the panel. I have what we did upstairs its folded up in a cupboard I know exactly where it is I've known where it is these past twenty-five years what is it now, twenty-six? It is upstairs it is there now I live with a quilt it is unfinished but I live with it. What is the difference why am I afraid I should go.

OK let's go then. When I make a decision that is it. Hat scarf bomber. My keys that were Jerry's keys. The light has moved up already it's out from the front window it's heading overhead it should be on the garden soon it will never be on the garden again. Leave. Lock the door. 1 Nova Scotia House my home Jerry's home it should be made of light it now has none.

    Wait for a bus it goes all round the houses. There's a train it goes direct but I can't afford it. The bus takes for ever what is for ever I'm used to it. What is it he said in that film, Hold me for ever, something like that, some bullshit, what trap are you in if you need for ever, if you need a lie of eternity, what can't you face, you cannot face how things are, it's so obvious, we live in the finite the day-to-day why hide. The bus takes for ever it's fine. The bus heads east and then further east, flatlands where no one wants to live, except someone forced offices here someone forced towers, obscene high rises obscene height, suddenly a cluster, sudden wealth sudden power, and so those who worked for obscene wealth obscene power moved this way too, started to live this way, but then that wealth got bored, that wealth realized it could make more wealth somewhere else, could make more wealth by having no offices, no tower, by being nowhere, stateless, no responsibilities, no burdens, shed everything, who cares about those towers, now they stand there, no one wants them, why would anyone want them, it's like lost space out here, lost time, communities that did not want to be occupied, then occupied, now deserted, the scars left, the communities not the same, they cannot just carry on, communities forgotten, communities dealing with the burdens left behind. We're here I am nowhere. Get off the bus. Wait there's a sign UK AIDS MEMORIAL QUILT EXHIBITION there's an arrow I am here.

I am crying I am not even in the place and I am crying. Let it come let it happen what am I going to do. Just breathe just breathe you don't have to go in you can go home it's OK it's OK. Go in, it's OK. I do not want to see it I do not want to be here. It's OK, go in. It's an exhibition centre it's big it's warm there are people it's OK. Feel old feel so timid feel so small. I need care I need Jerry. A lifetime ago, life. Where is the entrance here is the entrance. Some text on the wall.

UK AIDS MEMORIAL QUILT

The UK AIDS Memorial Quilt is a unique and irreplaceable historical document which tells the stories of approximately 384 people from all around the UK lost in the early days of the HIV and AIDS epidemic. The Quilts were made in the 1980s and 1990s with each panel commemorating someone who has died of AIDS and have been lovingly made by their friends, lovers and families.

Since the introduction of medications in the late 1990s people diagnosed with HIV can lead long and healthy lives. People living with HIV still encounter stigma and in the UK, 1 in 6 people are unaware of their HIV status.

The quilt is a remembrance of all those we have lost, a reminder of how far we've come in the fight against HIV and of how much there is still to do.

Open the door. There is so much it is so much. The space is like a warehouse. An aircraft hangar. The floor is covered in the quilts. So many. Panel and then panel and then panel. I am crying I am crying it's OK. Now is then, then is now, I am here.

Our Chris

The Lad

MARCH 1961 – JANUARY 1988

THE RIGHT TO LIVE

THE RIGHT TO BREATHE

THE RIGHT TO STAND BY

ALL THE THINGS

THAT I BELIEVE

MICHAEL!

your last name is sewn underneath
the strip.
perhaps one day your family will
re-learn
their pride
in you
and allow it to be shown. Until then
you will be known by these last
names........

MICHAEL THE GLASS ACT.
MICHAEL THE KIND.
MICHAEL THE SMILE.
MICHAEL THE MISSED.

Dear Scott,
I miss you so much!
Love,
Marc.

MALCOLM
I WISH THAT
I HAD KNOWN
YOU
LONGER

Colin Higgins

"Each person is different, never existed before, and never to exist again."

So many there are so many. Some just a name some just an image some with more, this one check cloth EDDIE it says red at the top, 6.7.57–7.6.91 at the bottom, in the panel a white sheet, written on it

My son.
My son.
Now you are gone
My memories of you
Still linger on.
My thoughts are with
you everyday
Ever since you
passed away.
Love you always.
Mum.

Next to it a red sheet on it in gold

IN THE NAME OF LOVE
LOVE NEVER DIES
S♥S

Nearby, a panel, fuchsia pink, in the centre a candle in a circle of rainbow. On the left it says

FOR THOSE
REJECTED
DENIED
ALONE

On the right:

'ANYONE'S DEATH DIMINISHETH ME . . .'

Crying and crying. It's OK. Going so slow. Read each one. I go so slow, I go so slow.

It's been an hour. I keep going to leave and then I stay I look again I look again. If Jerry had made it one more year just one more year maybe he could have survived maybe he would have survived maybe he would still be alive. I cannot think that way I cannot what will it do for me nothing what did it do for Jerry nothing. This is how it was this is how it is. Do not forget Jerry that is all I can do do not forget who he was what he did how he lived how to be. This is my guide this will always be my guide it is not messianic Jerry was human it's OK this will be my guide. OK let's leave let's go. Say thank you to a volunteer at the door, thank you. They smile they say are you OK, I say, I'm OK, thank you for asking, thank you for doing this, thank you for making this happen. Get out my phone message Fiona.

– You still got that needle and thread?
I message. She hasn't seen she hasn't seen she's seen she's replying.

– Ha! Somewhere
– Why?

I message about the exhibition and she asks how I am and I say I'm OK and then I say
– Let's finish Jerry's quilt

             – Yes let's
          – Come over. I'm free
           – Still can't sew

– Me neither.
– I'll be a couple of hours

              – All good
       – You know I'm not going anywhere

Go outside. The air is the air before yet the air so different. Get to the bus stop no one else waiting no sign of a bus no display board it's OK I can wait it's nothing I'm with my thoughts I'm with Jerry. Wherever I go I have this I have my love it's OK. This is the day this is the time in the day it passes that is how it is however long time may be. Finally, home. The panel is where I thought it was it's been there all along, the panel and a bag of material. Walk to Fiona's.

 Fiona's not been OK Fiona is getting better. Fiona opens the door Fiona smiles Fiona's face warm Fiona looks like she has been crying. Fiona's partner Rosie died three years ago, three years this summer, cancer.

 Come in Johnny, she says, we hug. I'm a mess, she says. Sorry, she says.

 Her flat is the same as it has always been like there is everything there and yet there is hardly anything there. She took out walls there is light there is space, a chair a table a sofa a daybed books on bookshelf three paintings by Jerry ceramics on shelves they were made by Rosie. The flat is not big but she has made it feel like space. When Rosie was alive it felt like they both had enough space. The place worked and they worked. After Rosie died Fiona said to me, look at us now, both widows.

She had designed her own kitchen she had built her own kitchen, with Rosie. Wood and iron and concrete and specifics and love.

Shall we be hopeless, Fiona says. She has opened a bottle of wine. I unpack the quilt, not even half finished, nothing like the ones I've just seen, it looks nothing like a wild garden a wild party. God look at it, she says. I am crying Fiona is crying. But Fiona is also laughing, she is crying she is laughing, god we were useless, she says, Jerry would have screamed at us.

I would say we were ambitious, I say.

I mean it's apt, says Fiona. Jerry's parties usually ended up a shit show.

We give up on trying to make it look like anything what we did already can just be the background, it's OK, the idea of it is there, even having the idea of it leaves the sense of it. We cut out a J an E an R another R a Y. I tell her of my day I tell her of the quilts I cry I talk I tell her, it helps. We talk about Jerry, we always talk about Jerry, Jerry is there with us always in everything. Talk of Jerry leads to talk of everything. I tell her about the flat the tower the light I tell her about my life, it helps. We are on the sofa the quilt between us I am on the J and Fiona is on the Y. I ask Fiona how she is.

I'm a shell of a human being, she says. It's over for me, I am done. I do more admin than I do teaching.

Fiona teaches at the school of architecture, she's been there for ever.

My whole day is admin. I'm called a lecturer but I'm an administrator I don't know why we pretend. And they have this way where I am made to feel bad about the admin that I am doing, like I'm not doing enough admin I could be doing more. Johnny I'm 67. I do not want to do admin. I want to teach. I do not know why I should continue.

Fiona is on the right-hand side of the right-hand diagonal of the top of the Y. I am trying to be as neat as I can with the curve of the J but I cannot be neat with the curve of the J I'm sorry Jerry I cannot be neat.

What would Jerry say to you, I ask Fiona.

You know I always think that, Fiona says, what would Jerry say to me. Jerry would say, you know what you should do, but can you face it?

And what would he mean?

Get. The. Fuck. Out.

Fiona is staring at me her mouth is open like she has just inhaled shock oxygen. And then her mouth falls maybe because my mouth falls, faces mimic each other, it is how we communicate, really, not words, her face falls, my face falls.

When I think of Jerry, says Fiona, I think of him so old, but now here I am older than he ever was, older than Rosie ever was.

I'm about the age Jerry was, I say.

You are so young.

You are so young, Fiona.

Fiona is going down the inside of the top of the Y. I am round the curve of the J going up to the horizontal line.

Fiona finishes the Y. OK an R, she says. There was what between us, twelve years? Jerry died eleven years after my first friend died of AIDS. Andrew. There was a year I went to fourteen funerals. There was so much death, and grief. It changes you. It changed me. Then I feel guilty for thinking about myself.

Fiona is on the curve of the R. I am finishing the J I finish the J. I go onto the E.

It changed me utterly, Fiona says, it hardened me. And yet now I am meant to carry on as normal, as if nothing happened. It pushed me inward. Remember when we first met, Johnny? That night, that party. I was done. How could I carry on after what we had lived through. How can we live? What conditions do we need to be able to live? That was my path. Theory not practice. That was how I could continue, because I could not carry on as normal. And so here I am, 67, an architect who has never built. My interventions have been slight, the interiors of places, like this place. And this was with Rosie.

Would you like to build, I say.

Yes, she says. But there is the impossibility of building. Building well and with purpose and without compromise. And I never want to build anything like that.

She points out of her window to a new build a few blocks away, where the Albion used to be, a building that is like a cube dumped on the skyline, an aggressive block of weight, like it's been dumped on top of what is already there, this cube that has no purpose just a pretence of luxury.

You have taught people, I say.

I know that and I understand that. I don't diminish that or downplay that. But what does it mean to teach now when if I was a kid I could not afford to go to college. How can I teach the impossibility of building in the impossibility of education?

Her R is fiddly her R is complete she starts on the middle R. I am still on E.

Which brings us to the impossibility of living, Fiona says. Being within the impossibility of living, facing it, not hiding from it, not masking it, I am ready to live.

You sound like Jerry, I say.

He taught me.

Fiona sews I sew.

We are silent we are silent we sew I am thinking I say what I think. What do you think Jerry would have been doing now, I say.

He wouldn't be here, says Fiona.

In this room? I say.

In this city, in this country, he'd be gone. Johnny, it might be hard to hear but I have always thought he settled down with you because he was sick. He loved you and I do not ever want to diminish that love. But I have always wondered what Jerry would have done if he had not got sick, or if he'd just lasted one damn more year, if he'd just kept going, he missed antiretrovirals by, what, months. If he'd just kept going he may well have survived. But he couldn't he didn't know none of us knew. What can you do. But if he hadn't got sick, if he'd survived, if he could have lived undetectable, he wouldn't have hung around. He would have needed his freedom. He always loved that you had your freedom. I'm sorry Johnny but I do not think he would be with you.

You think.

Yes I think. It's hard but it's what I think. He was free. He was always free. We must remember him as free.

I think so too, I say, and I am crying but it is a relief to say it, to think it. Jerry is free. Togetherness, aloneness, not loneliness, wholeness, fire. That is what he gives me if I can see it if I can face it.

We must live with our wounds, Fiona is saying, the wounds that are so open to us, so raw, but others do not see our wounds, others want us to move on, and to forget. Others want us to seek comfort in forgetting. To seek solace in forgetting. To forget would be to assimilate. We live with our wounds they never close.

We sew we sew we are silent we are within ourselves with each other, Fiona with Rosie, me with Jerry, Jerry my love my wound my all. I am sewing I am sewing. I do not know where I can go I do not know what to do.

There, Fiona says, finished.

15

Things happen quickly. Gareth could no longer cope in his flat Gareth couldn't handle the stairs. Gareth had a niece who had a farm. He hardly ever left his flat and now he could not leave the flat and so he had to leave. I was round there checking in on him. You know my niece Megan, he said, Gareth had spoken of her often, Megan was a farmer, Megan was hardcore. She's going to take me in. Then Gareth said, she's finished with her girlfriend, she wants to change everything. Then Gareth said, I was talking with Megan about Fiona, she said she'd like to meet her.

Gareth was all energy all planned out all set all certain. Four decades I have been in this flat, Gareth said, five decades in this city. This flat and this city have been my home, and they have taught me the meaning of home. Maybe now it is time to return home, and to finally be myself at home.

Gareth was silent for a while, I let the silence sit. Of course I never want to set foot in the house where I was a child ever again, he said eventually. How meaningless, how pointless, it is from these places that we flee. Now when I say home, I do not mean a building, a predefined space, a space predefined by others into which I was meant to fit in. Now what I mean by home is the land where I came from, the air the light. It is e-le-men-tal.

I was jealous I wanted what Gareth wanted I wanted what was elemental. I never told him I was jealous but I think he knew I'd be jealous I think he knew what he was doing. Friendship is often tempered jealousy. Is jealousy good I don't know but it was the spur it was the kick I am not used to change I need to change. Who is going to look after you, I said, and, you need someone to look after you, and, I can come and look after you.

Gareth smiled and he said but you're so young and he said but you have so much life to live and he said, why do you want to waste your time on a ghost like me. It was what Jerry said to me all that time ago it was the same then as it is now it's not even a question or at least it is not a question for me this is living life. What else am I going to do let's see what happens let's go.

We made plans. Gareth told Fiona, Fiona got in touch with Megan. One Saturday we set off for a visit. Fiona drove us Gareth was in the front I was in the back. The drive was meant to be five hours sixteen minutes it took us over seven. We drove we drove motorway then a bridge an endless bridge over an estuary a bridge that had to begin and end deep inland to find solid ground. Motorway, main road, then, for an hour, a road often of single track over hills. We arrived, the farm, the sea.

Megan was there Megan was smiling. It is so good to see you, she said to Gareth, how are you holding up. Sitting down for seven hours straight is pretty run of the mill for me, said Gareth, I'm doing fine. Gareth introduced us, Hello,

Megan said to me, and then to Fiona, it's so good to meet you in person.

The whole journey Fiona told us about her phone and email conversations with Megan. She has all these old buildings that have been out of use for years, she said, modern machinery is just too big for them, she said. Megan had been going in circles with her old girlfriend ever decreasing circles she said she had been trapped. She sounded a nightmare. Megan wants to make up for lost time Megan wants to restore Megan wants to repurpose Megan wants to build.

Megan had food ready it was glorious. We ate we talked but really Fiona and Megan talked, and then Fiona and Megan went off. Gareth smiled and Gareth just said, maybe good things can happen.

Gareth could still walk with some help and some care. We went out he showed me the land it was glorious. There was the farm there was the sea there was the standing stones, in the next field, six stones holding up one stone on top, ancient burial chamber, Gareth said. We leant against the stones, Gareth needed to rest, we looked out to sea. Do you think you could live here, said Gareth. Maybe, I said. I'm scared and I'm terrified so maybe I think it is good.

We talked and we talked and then Gareth said I should keep going down the path and see what's round the corner, he was happy there by the stones he would wait. And so I set off, down a path to a cliff that turns into a bay, in which is a small village I mean barely a village, as many houses as there are flats in Nova Scotia House. That was it.

We stayed the night I slept and I slept. The air was mine it was mine. The next morning the weather was in it was hard to see anything. Breakfast was delicious we helped to cook we helped to prepare the table we helped to wash up. The wing of the cottage was all ground floor. It is perfect for me, said Gareth.

Megan and Fiona talked us through their plans but really they were talking with each other about their plans, re-iterating them to each other once more. There could be studios, they said. There could be living quarters, they said. Meeting spaces, they said. One building was like a bunker built into the hill. This could be for parties, they said. We'll soundproof it. This can be for your vegetables, they said to me. You are a gardener you have always been a gardener you can garden.

More plans, this time how to live. Everybody would work everybody would contribute through their work that is how they would pay their way. Some could live permanently some could come for residences, artist studios performance studios recording studios. Come stay come make come work on the land. Megan would keep running the farm. Grow produce make produce sell produce. We talked we talked we were alive.

Johnny do you remember when Jerry drew that farm, said Gareth, do you remember. I remembered I always remembered I lit up that Gareth remembered. I still have the drawing, I said. We should frame it, said Gareth, for here. I think about what he drew all the time, I said to Gareth. Me too, Gareth said. It is what Jerry wanted, for himself, for us. Let us do it let's see if it works. When we lived in the warehouses we did not know what we were doing. We don't know what we are doing but we know why we want to try. So let us do this now.

I am in, Fiona said.

What about Johnny, said Gareth.

And so I said yes and so that was the start of whatever this is.

Gareth said he had a life of savings Gareth said he could sell his flat in seconds Gareth said he'd bought it for thirty grand Gareth said he'd now get for it what six hundred thousand. Gareth said he'd get it cash.

Megan gave Fiona the plans Fiona started sketching Fiona started measuring Fiona looked at light Fiona talked with Megan the two of them a unit already the two of them looking at buildings looking at walls looking at space. Gareth and I sat inside by a fire Gareth a blanket over his legs. I checked my phone, one guy five miles away, another thirteen miles away. But then a guy messaged, hi, he said, hi, I said, nice pic, he said, thanks, I said, likewise, I said. Are you around, he said, not right now, I said, maybe soon.

We drove back, all talk all the way, Fiona asking Gareth about the warehouses how they lived what they constructed how it was. Life is different now everything is different now we can be the same as we were then, said Gareth. When we got back we had already begun. Fiona started making plans. Fiona had never built Fiona now wanted to build. Fiona would message

– Come round Saturday Megan is visiting let's talk about spaces and then
– not just spaces we think we need but how we can exist in spaces how spaces exist for us

                                        and then
                            — queering space haha
   — OK sure
I wrote back.
   — How are you feeling
                                        — Like I'm 27
                                            she said.

   I handed in my notice. I messaged Liz I said I would be leaving the city I would no longer need the flat. Liz replied, oh no, and, are you OK, and I told all. We set a date when I would be out. And then she said, do you know anyone else who would be interested in subletting. I asked Irene at the surgery and she said her grandson Tyrone. It is like we are our own local council.
   Once a decision is made that's it. It is the only way to be. When Jerry asked me to move in that was it I moved in. I was with Jerry that was it. I move out now that is it. Grew up in a village no shop one bus out a day it is normal for me. What is normal.
   Gareth has moved there already why wait, he said. Sold his flat the day it went on the market. Cash buyer, over asking price. I helped him pack up but really it was easy everything was so ordered so exact. Gareth packed up what he wanted Gareth sold what he didn't want that was it. It's all gone, said Gareth, good. As it should be. Let us renew.
   They drove off. Maude with him Maude already rules the place. Fiona has kept her place Fiona is not done with the city Fiona wants both. I've been taking a minute to move I've been taking my time. I've been at the farm often I've dug

I've started to prepare the soil. Megan never had the time for a kitchen garden the soil needs care the soil needs some love. Luckily I have manure, she said.

Some crops I've put in straight away potatoes carrots onions leaves marrow strawberries raspberries herbs. The work will take years the build the reimagining, we may never be finished, Fiona says. The immediate work is Gareth's quarters, flattening and smoothing the floor widening the doors, intuitive design of living, how do humans exist what do we need. What do we really need, not what we are conditioned to want. Gareth's quarters and then other spaces for living, spaces for living that are also spaces for working and making, Fiona imposing little on these spaces except what is needed. It's up to the individual to decide how to be in the space, said Fiona, it's not for me to tell them. I mean really what do I need, a bed, light, warmth, that's it.

Here in Nova Scotia House the tower now blocks the light the garden does not know what to do. Pot up what I can, take cuttings from what I can. Some plants will make the move easily some won't survive the shock. I'll take what I can, maybe some won't like the soil there anyway maybe some won't like the exposure maybe some will miss the heat from these buildings these people this city maybe some will flourish maybe some will feel relief. I won't miss the city because there's nothing to miss I can come down anytime crash on someone's floor or maybe just stay out no sleep there's always someone somewhere.

Pot up, pack. Let me sort through who I am, who I have been, who I could be. Jerry's paintings are off the wall, they are packed they are ready. Stones and stones and stones, most I cannot take, stones Jerry had gathered through his life, stones we gathered together, most I do not know their story I do not know where they are from, Jerry never told me Jerry would not remember himself, that is not the point, the stones were gathered the stones came and gave witness here the stones will stay. Plants come out of the garden stones take their place, edges lined with stones, paths, the stones they will remain I will collect more stones on the beach below the farm, Jerry would love it there, he would love what we were doing. Who knows if he would love what we were doing maybe he'd think we were crazy maybe he'd think we were naïve, who knows who can know. My version of Jerry, my Jerry in my head in my body in my blood, my Jerry always with me, that Jerry loves what we are doing, that Jerry loves the farm the isolation the possibility, that is enough.

    Jerry's diaries, our letters, our paper trail, they are coming with me. Here's one, a letter Jerry wrote to me, his first hospital stay,

My <u>dear</u> Johnny

    It is four in the morning, I cannot sleep and so I am writing to you. I am so scared, my Johnny, I am so afraid. I hate to say this to you maybe I won't send this letter maybe I will throw it in the trash where it belongs where I belong.

    I am so scared and so afraid. I do not want to be scared I do not want to be afraid. It helps just to write these words Johnny it helps me. If it's OK with you I will send this letter it helps me to know these words will be read. I will tell you when I see you later to not take this letter seriously when it arrives. I <u>love</u> you Johnny. You will go on I will not know you. You will know me, you will know what I was I hope I am enough for you I hope I have been enough. It's 5.33 now Johnny. I dozed for a moment. Dawn has begun you are how many miles from me how far. I do not know distance all I know is that you are <u>here with me always</u>. Johnny it is so cruel. The light is coming outside I can see trees the tops of trees that's all there is.

Please don't be scared by my words please don't be frightened I love you Johnny I love you.

Your old silly fool

Jerry

When he wrote it he was younger than I am now. How is it to be with bones this age the bones of my body this age the flesh, it all still functioning, like Jerry's should be functioning, like Jerry should be now. How is it to be this age how to keep free how to keep out of the trap and the traps. Jerry warned me do not get trapped do not. Traps can be overt traps can be obvious, the guy whose name I do not know, an obvious trap, for me anyway, maybe for some other guy he'd be synergy, for me a trap never again I need something other. That is an overt trap but sometimes other traps are hidden they are not clear they are not obvious until you are in the trap caught by the trap, sentimentality is a trap, acquiescence is a trap, compromise is a trap, complicity is a trap, normality is a trap. I am leaving here that is it goodbye Nova Scotia House goodbye. It is not about feeling young it is not about pretending to be anything than what I am this human this age these memories these possibilities.

It is all being picked up tomorrow the plants our books our records are coming. Plates are coming, some are from the warehouses, they've survived this long, they will come to our new world. Our cups, straight edged for coffee, curved mugs for tea. The furniture, the sofa, the chair, the headboard of our bed, all of Michael's pieces are coming. One hundred and twenty-seven paintings by Jerry all packed and ready. Tomorrow the van comes we pack the van I will lock the door I will hand over the key goodbye number 1 Nova Scotia House. You were never mine. The pull of Jerry inside me is tidal gravitational moon-powered, a pull a constant pull, being by the sea will help me. The pull is there it is always there I do not want to go I will go.

Last time I was at the farm what five days ago I was digging I was digging I was covering weeded ground with tarp. It was hot but the breeze from the sea worked for me. I was in cut-off jeans that was it. I looked at my phone a guy nine miles away no one else anywhere close. And then there was a message, hey. Nice smile nice eyes, said he was 38. Two miles away. Where are you, I said. He said, at sea. He said, lol. He said, coming ashore soon. He said, what are you up to later?

I said, what are you doing at sea, he said, working. He said, where are you at, I said I was on the farm, he said, oh you're one of them. I said yes I'm one of them. He said, I'm pretty much level with you now, he said, come to the cliff.

Ha, I said, OK, I said. I went down the hill I went past the standing stones I got to the cliff there was this little fishing boat flat-bottomed rectangular motor powered no cover a steering wheel on it this guy in orange coveralls pushed off the shoulder tied at the waist a black T-shirt he was pulling up a basket I messaged look up. I watched him pull up the basket I watched him empty it I watched him put it back. He worked and then he looked at his phone and he looked up and he saw me and he waved. He had a beard he had no beard in his photo that was OK. He pointed to the village and then he messaged, meet me in the port, and so I walked into the estuary down the cliff I walked the same speed as his boat. I was looking he was looking I walked to the village he steered his boat to the village. I stood on the beach he came to the shore. He jumped out he said hey I said hey I helped him pull his boat up to shore I helped him pack up his boat. He's called Barney. We went off to his I'm seeing him again tomorrow that's really all there is to say.

Appendix: The History of the Quilt

The UK AIDS Memorial Quilt is a unique historical document, paying tribute to approximately 384 UK residents who died of AIDS in the 1980s and 90s. The Quilt was the initiative of Alistair Hume, who had been inspired by the US AIDS Quilt, founded by activist Cleve Jones. In the late 80s, Hume met Jones in San Francisco and saw the US Quilt, known as the Names Project. On his return to Edinburgh, Hume set up a UK chapter, one of sixty-two chapters around the world.

Each panel is approximately 6 feet by 3 feet, representing the size of a grave plot. At the time, many of those who died of AIDS did not receive funerals, owing both to stigma within families and funeral homes refusing to handle the bodies. By making a panel, those who had died could be memorialized by friends, lovers, communities and enlightened family members.

Once a panel had been made, it was sent to the UK office of the Names Project in Edinburgh, with documentation about who the panel was for, and its maker. Memorabilia was also sometimes included. These panels were then stitched together to create blocks measuring 12 feet by 12 feet. As the Quilt grew, it was often displayed around the country, including in Hyde Park in 1994, echoing a display of the US Quilt on the National Mall in Washington DC.

Each panel is unique, representing different quilt-making skills, techniques and modes of expression for the love, sorrow, grief, despair and anger felt by its makers. Many panels address continuing stigma over HIV/AIDS, including panels with names of the dead partially or entirely hidden at the insistence of bigoted family members. Quilt-making could help the bereaved through their grief. Some panels were started by those with HIV infection who knew they had little time left, overseeing how they were memorialized.

The UK Names Project folded in 1996, coinciding with the introduction of antiretroviral treatments, which made it possible to live a full life with an HIV+ status. The UK Quilt was eventually placed in storage, where it remained for several years without any conservation or care. In 2014, a partnership of volunteers from UK HIV charities formed to bring the Quilt back into the public consciousness. Today, the UK AIDS Memorial Quilt Partnership works to ensure its ongoing conservation and visibility, both to memorialize those who died and to fight continuing HIV stigma today. To learn more about the UK AIDS Memorial Quilt, and to donate, please visit www.aidsquiltuk.org.

Acknowledgements

It has been my honour to get to know Siobhán Lanigan and Clifford McManus, members of the UK AIDS Memorial Quilt Partnership. Their insight and support have been invaluable. I thank the Partnership, and I mourn those memorialized by the Quilt.

I started writing *Nova Scotia House* in May 2020, during the production of *What Artists Wear*. The book's first reader was Olivia Laing, who responded with energy, enthusiasm, encouragement, engagement: everything I needed.

Chloe Currens, my editor at Penguin, is incredible, immediately understanding the need to write fiction to tell this story. Thanks also to Thea Tuck at Penguin Press. Thank you to Sam Talbot, Isabel Davies, Gavin Read, Jodie Lewis. My agents Rebecca Carter and PJ Mark are the wisest and most deft stewards of work – thank you both. Thank you to Nicola Tyson for the cover image, and for your memories of that Thames foreshore visit.

Thanks to the staff of the British Library, particularly the librarians of Rare Books and Music, as well as all those whose labour in the building is unseen.

Thank you to Dan Beaumont and Morgan Clement, as well as the Chapter 10 Book Club: Harry Agius, Eve Dawoud,

Debi Ghose, Ali Gitlow, Luke Howard. I also thank Luke as part of Horse Meat Disco, alongside James Hillard, Severino Panzetta and Jim Stanton. Thank you to Gideon Berger and all the Block9 family. I pay tribute to the late David Pollard of the Joiners Arms, and send thanks to Dave Kendrick. Thank you to Princess Julia, who provided crucial insight, as well as to Hilton Als, Frances Armstrong-Jones, Laura and William Burlington, Paul Flynn, Chantal Joffe, Maureen Paley, Ajesh Patalay, Ann Stephenson, Alessio Vanetti, and the Friends of Arnold Circus.

    I send my love to my sisters, and their families, always.

    Richard Porter was with me when I finished the first draft, at 16.40 on 20 March 2024. It was sunset on the eve of the spring equinox: we got in the car, and took our dog Orpheus down to the sea, the beach pretty much ours alone for an hour of glory. Thank you, Rich.